Creative Capers From Scotland

Edited By Sarah Washer

First published in Great Britain in 2018 by:

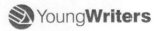 Young**Writers**

Young Writers
Remus House
Coltsfoot Drive
Peterborough
PE2 9BF
Telephone: 01733 890066
Website: www.youngwriters.co.uk

FOREWORD

Young Writers was created in 1991 with the express purpose of promoting and encouraging creative writing. Each competition we create is tailored to the relevant age group, hopefully giving each child the inspiration and incentive to create their own piece of work, whether it's a poem or a short story. We truly believe that seeing their work in print gives pupils a sense of achievement and pride in their work and themselves.

Every day children bring their toys to life, creating fantastic worlds and exciting adventures, using nothing more than the power of their imagination. What better subject then for primary school pupils to write about, capturing these ideas in a mini saga – a story of just 100 words. With so few words to work with, these young writers have really had to consider their words carefully, honing their writing skills so that every word counts towards creating a complete story.

Within these pages you will find stories about toys coming to life when we're not looking and tales of peril when toys go missing or get lost! Some young writers went even further into the idea of play and imagination, and you may find magical lands or fantastic adventures as they explore their creativity. Each one showcases the talent of these budding new writers as they learn the skills of writing, and we hope you are as entertained by them as we are.

CONTENTS

Danderhall Primary School, Danderhall

Lucie Reid (10)	56
Kaitlyn Munro (10)	57
Leo Wilson (10)	58
Maia Makorie (10)	59
Emma Kennedy (10)	60
Cameron Sean Peter Elliot (10)	61
Cassie Shaw (10)	62
Taylor Russell (10)	63

Kirkliston Primary School, Kirkliston

Emilie Thomson (10)	64
Leo Evans (9)	65
Siya Ramsohok (10)	66
Lucy Elder (10)	67
Sofia Robb (10)	68
Sophie Stewart (9)	69
Lanah Banks (10)	70
Aaron Michael McVeigh (10)	71
Gregor Burn (10)	72
Yoshua Mthokozisi Gordon (10)	73
Tom Ellaway (10)	74
Abigail Beth Mclean (9)	75
Albert Sienko (10)	76
Grace Ann Shedden (10)	77
Kara Mcneill (10)	78
Lucy Mclellan (10)	79
Ben Sansom (10)	80
Scarlett McGuire (10)	81
Yasmin Mutiara Hunter (10)	82
Fraser Innes Mitchell (10)	83
Morgan Middleton (10)	84
Aamna Mahmood (10)	85
Alice Reedie (9)	86
Carla Vaughan (10)	87
Rebecca Thorington (10)	88
Wang Sum Lo (10)	89
Blair Roberts (10)	90
Evan Ross (10)	91
Andrew Kerr (10)	92

Cameron Proudfoot (10)	93
Lucy Richmond (10)	94
Jamie Josh Sinclair (10)	95
Ruby Corson (10)	96
Brooke Thomson (10)	97
Léa Hogg (10)	98
Lewis Robert Alexander Briggs (10)	99
Calum Russell Gilmore (10)	100
Tymek Rusinek (10)	101
Ella Rutherford (9)	102
Thomas Kenneth Newport (10)	103

Langlands Primary School, Forfar

Corrina Amy Joan Hood (10)	104
Jodi Balfour (9)	105
Michaela Hart (8)	106
Eilidh Bisset (9)	107
Sophia Cameron (9)	108
Willow Forrester (9)	109
Rebecca Anne Rebel Whitton (9)	110
Sophie Baikie (9)	111
Paul de Veres (9)	112
Bethany Young (10)	113
Maja Stokes (9)	114
Abbi Ewen (8)	115
Rhys Lawson (9)	116
Dominic Pye (9)	117
Owen Low (9)	118
Millie Stewart (9)	119
Brooke Greig (9)	120
Jessica Gibbs (9)	121
Hollie Stewart (9)	122
Molly Brown (9)	123
Charlie Davidson (9)	124

Milton Of Leys Primary School, Milton Of Leys

Sheonagh Mitchell (10)	125
Euan Douglas Learmonth (10)	126
Katie Strachan (10)	127
Rhea Williams (10)	128

Molly Fitzpatrick (10)	129	Jayden Long (8)	169
Lucy Mia McGibbon (10)	130	Ross Middleton (9)	170
Mia Croall (10)	131	Kayden Netherington (8)	171
Cara Cuthbert (10)	132	Millie Roache (8)	172
Kirstie Munro (10)	133		
Carla Quigley (10)	134		
Chloe Ironside (10)	135		
Aimee Cameron (10)	136		
Ben Murdoch (10)	137		
Shaun Clare (10)	138		
Zach Evans (10)	139		
Jamie Hamilton (10)	140		
Karlis Rozenbahs (10)	141		
Ethan Allan Rae (10)	142		
Rachel Sharp (9)	143		
Neve Crawford (10)	144		
Cole Cameron (10)	145		
Emma Bowsher (10)	146		
Sam Kinnear (10)	147		
Theo Cartwright (10)	148		
Sophia Loates (10)	149		
Christopher Buchanan (10)	150		
Caleb Dowling (10)	151		
Joel Sleet (10)	152		
Keryn Maclean (10)	153		
Calvin Barrie Cornthwaite (10)	154		
Owen Anderson (10)	155		
Keira Broadfoot (10)	156		
Tristan Crook (10)	157		

Portlethen Primary School, Portlethen

Eilah Sophie Win (9)	173
Jacob Arthur Saum (9)	174
Lewis Scotson (10)	175
Lola Phillips-Johns (10)	176
Andrew Liam Brown (9)	177
Lacey May Murray (11)	178
Alex Proszynski (9)	179
Eva Brownie (10)	180
Ellis J Harrison (9)	181
Sophia Le Tissier (9)	182
Miya Skea Bowes (9)	183
Owen Smith (10)	184
Lewis Benjamin Archibald (9)	185
Lewis Riddoch (9)	186

Our Lady's RC Primary School, Perth

Callum Mckay (9)	158
Sophie Rigby (8)	159
Jan Jaromir Kruczynski (8)	160
Shayla Mangan (9)	161
Karolina Maraszkiewicz (8)	162
Laura-Marie Barzey (9)	163
Chloe Geddes (9)	164
Ben Brown (8)	165
Ciara Rowe (8)	166
Maddy Taylor (8)	167
Jack Anderson (8)	168

St Dominic's Primary School, Airdrie

Rhys Deighan (11)	187
Aiden Heafey (11)	188
Szymon Kisiel (11)	189
Dawid Tomalka (11)	190
John Michael Sweeney (11)	191
Rhys Brannan (11)	192
Michael Hunt (11)	193
Marco Russo (10)	194
Leah Hamilton (11)	195
Ethan McGee (11)	196
Rhys McCarthy Railley (11)	197
Kai Stewart (11)	198
Leah McCabe (11)	199
Kerry McGill (11)	200
Jamie Shaw (11)	201

St Patrick's Primary School, New Stevenston

Liam Dunnery (8)	202
Josh Hutchison (8)	203
Aiden Clarke (7)	204
Maksymilian Jablonski (8)	205
Nikkita McAviney (8)	206
Lisa McMonagle (8)	207
Emmanuel Mathew (7)	208
Allanah Hall (8)	209
Blair Carlyle (8)	210
Hannah Margaret Doyle (7)	211

THE MINI SAGAS

Mummy Love

Once, there was a girl named Lucy. She had a teddy which she called Rose. It was her favourite teddy. At night everybody was asleep so Rose escaped to find her family. She searched the house and found a photo. She went and found a dark place and cried and cried. She walked very slowly up the stairs. Then she went and looked in Lucy's Mum and Dad's room and jumped on the bed. She cried a bit more. Then heard somebody say, "Are you okay?"

Rose recognised that voice and said, "Mummy," and lived happily ever after.

Macy Ruby Screen (8)

Balmoral Primary School, Galashiels

Pokémon's Friends

Once upon a time, there was a Pokémon called Mew who lived in a dungeon with nothing to eat. A door opened and a Pokémon called Mewtwo appeared. Mewtwo said, "We need to get out of here, let's go." They went out into the wildlife. They got to Mewtwo's home and ate Pooke-Puffles and went to bed. Mew slept next to the fire.

In the morning they woke up and then they heard a roar and it was Groudon, the biggest Pokémon in the world, they made friends and they all lived happily together.

Faye Campbell (8)
Balmoral Primary School, Galashiels

Teddy

All was quiet that night then Teddy woke up. She tried to wake the other toys but nothing happened so she kissed and cuddled them and it worked. Teddy was so excited she could shout, but the other toys said, "Do not shout." They all had a party and danced. Teddy and the other toys were hungry so they went to the kitchen to get some sweets and chocolate and ate them all. The other toys heard a noise so they went to go and investigate, but it was only Teddy's stomach, happy and full.

Rebecca Scott (8)
Balmoral Primary School, Galashiels

The Biscuit Doll

Once, there was a doll called Dream. She was locked in the kitchen and she was very hungry so she looked in the cupboard for biscuits. Finally, she found some so she ate. Then she ran out of biscuits so she made more. When she made them she ran out of chocolate to make more. So she played in the garden for five and a half hours. She got her fluffy pyjamas with sheep on them and watched Horrid Henry till ten o'clock, then she had a bag of marshmallows and then she went to bed and slept.

Brooke Gunn (8)
Balmoral Primary School, Galashiels

Patches The Cheetah

One day Kayla went to school. While Kayla was at school, Patches the teddy felt lonely. So Patches jumped off the white desk and went downstairs into the living room and saw the colourful fish having fun. Patches decided to jump in the fish tank. The fish gave Patches a swimming lesson. After the swimming lesson, Patches got hungry so Patches ate all the fish. When Kayla got home she was surprised that the fish were gone. Then she found her cheetah lying near the fish tank, wet.

Kayla Gibb (7)
Balmoral Primary School, Galashiels

The Space Battle

When Jack was asleep every night, war was happening around his bed. Han Solo glided his Millennium Falcon around the bedroom, he enjoyed shooting the Stormtroopers. Luke Skywalker was helping him with his lightsaber, the Stormtroopers were toys so they never died. Darth Vader came out from under the bed. He tried to stop Han Solo from killing his soldiers. Jack's alarm went off and all the toys froze. "That's weird," said Jack, "all my toys have moved."

Jack Wright (7)
Balmoral Primary School, Galashiels

The Lego Man

There was a Lego character in Fearne's bed. He liked to hide then cause trouble.

One day, when the dark house was empty, the Lego man put toilet paper everywhere. It was hanging from the lights covering Fearne's brother's bed and wrapped around the TV. While this was going on Bonnie the dog was watching with her paws over her eyes. Fearne's mum came home early, she thought the dog has been naughty and gave her a row. The Lego man smiled, watching Bonnie cry.

Fearne Eva Louise Miller (8)
Balmoral Primary School, Galashiels

The Robot Dragon

In Toys World War I, there was a big battle. From space, a really big rock bashed into the ground because the toys fought each other, the dragon didn't know who were the good guys so he was scared.

But five years later he won and he made a tomb so every toy was safe, but not for long. A dino came and bashed and roared and stomped. The robot dragon tried to stop it so the toys didn't get hurt, but he got hurt. He was nice to the dino and it's his pet.

Robert Dalgliesh (8)

Balmoral Primary School, Galashiels

The Bad Unicorn

One day, when Emily went to school, Sparkles the bad unicorn jumped off the desk and onto the bed. She was feeling naughty, using her horn, she changed all the teddies black. The teddies were crying big, fat tears. Next, they started to scream but she would not let them get down. Suddenly, one huge wet tear dripped on her from a teddy's face, so she turned them back and said sorry. Emily's mum was confused at why the carpet was wet and salty...

Emily Gilbertson (8)
Balmoral Primary School, Galashiels

Bad Whisper Boy

Once, there was a boy called James. He was walking to school. He saw a stand with teddies so he got a teddy but when he got home he was playing with it, but his dad said, "Come down to get your tea, it is ready." But when he was having his tea he was watching a scary movie, but his teddy moved his head, then he went to bed, then the teddy whispered in his ear. When he woke up, the teddy punched him in the eye, then he gave it back to the boy.

Daylon Jeffrey (7)
Balmoral Primary School, Galashiels

The Nasty Barbie Doll

Once upon a time, there was a wonderful Barbie doll that lived in a fantastic castle. She was extremely nasty, she bossed the other toys about. She screamed and lost her voice until they ignored her. Then the toys enjoyed having fun. They all had a musical party, then a wicked witch entered the room and turned the amazing music off and said a spell. They all froze and because the fire was on, they all melted like ice into a puddle on the floor.

Brooke Donaldson (7)
Balmoral Primary School, Galashiels

The Adventure

Mr Longlegs, the toy spider, loved adventures. He had climbed every tree in the forest, made thousands of webs and swam in every river. What he really wanted to do though was to get out of the forest and explore the world, but he was made of fluff.

One day, on his travels, he found a toy car and drove it out, got on the motorway with lots of big, fast cars. Sadly, one ran over him. That was the end of Mr Longlegs' travels.

Kenzie McLaughlin (8)
Balmoral Primary School, Galashiels

Spider-Man And The Cat

Fast Spider-Man waited until no one was at home. He was hiding in the bathroom shooting webs in the wall. A black cat was sleeping on the bed then Spider-Man woke him up. Spider-Man jumped on the cat's back. The cat woke up and started running around the room. The cat was scared. Spider-Man was having lots of fun.
After five minutes the cat was tired and fell asleep, cuddled up with his new friend.

Jack Thomson (7)
Balmoral Primary School, Galashiels

Battle Plane

One day a mini battle plane came to life and then flew out the window to the garden. The battle plane engine ran out of power. The plane exploded. The explosion started a fire in a nearby tree. The fire spread across the fence and up the side of the house. Reilly woke up to find his house on fire and firemen putting it out. He could not understand why his plane was in the tree...

Reilly Pearson (7)
Balmoral Primary School, Galashiels

One Stormy Night

One stormy night, a toy unicorn woke up and started singing. Her voice was like an angel. The other toys watched her but were crying. She asked why they were sad. They said, "We want to sing like you." She taught them how to sing like angels. They made a concert. All the teddy bears sang. All the toys were happy and they sang every night afterwards.

Millie Rose Devlin (7)
Balmoral Primary School, Galashiels

Darth Teddy Wars

One day Darth Teddy woke up alone. There were no people, so he thought he would be naughty. He started to kick the other teddies. He pulled the teddies' arms off. He said lots of bad swear words. The teddies covered their ears. One teddy had a plan, she sat on him and a different teddy took out his voice. He could never talk again, but learnt to be good.

Kyle Daniel Patterson (8)
Balmoral Primary School, Galashiels

The One Hundred Lego Man

Once, a small Lego man was in a car race on a racing track. He thought he was going to lose and he was right. He crashed hard into a yellow racing car. He was rushed to hospital in an ambulance. Sadly, he had to get his arm cut off because it was so bad.

Two months later, he raced again, he won first place and won £10,000.

Cole Logan Sands (8)
Balmoral Primary School, Galashiels

Santa's Express

It's Christmas Eve. I'm Oscar and I'm a Beanie Boo. I'm so excited because I'm in Santa's house and Mrs Claus invited me to their house. I was having a lovely hot chocolate with Mrs Claus and some mince pies. I feel spoilt! I'm helping Santa deliver the presents all around the world. Suddenly, Santa pulled the brake and I fell out of the sleigh. I was holding hands with another toy and he was called Pinky. Suddenly, we broke hands because Santa split the sleigh in half! I landed in Hogwarts. We cast Christmas spells and stayed for Christmas.

Isla Nimmo (8)
Callander Primary School, Bridgend

Ziggi's Adventure

It's Christmas Eve and my name's Ziggi. I'm a toy alien. Tonight is a very special night because I heard the elves say I'll be taken to London! The time is 5pm, I'm about to go to Santa Claus' house for departure. Suddenly, I was in the sky on the sleigh. The wind gushes right behind me. Suddenly I went *whoosh*, and I flew out of the sleigh and tumbled down! Another toy fell down with me, then I was on the top of the Christmas tree of Liberty of London. Finally, I popped into Liberty of London advent calendar.

Stewart Douglas Watson (8)
Callander Primary School, Bridgend

Strictly Come Dancing With Barbie!

It's Christmas Eve and my name is Barbie. I'm getting delivered to my owner and I'm so excited to go to my new home. "I love this sleigh," I said to Santa.
He said, "Ho, ho, ho!" I loved the sound of the bells. Suddenly, I fell off the sleigh and I landed in Blackpool in the Blackpool ballroom. With 'Strictly Come Dancing' and I was really loving it! I fell onto Debbie and Giovanni! They were spinning around and around! I was really dizzy! Next Katya and Joe did an exquisite dance! Santa saw me and we flew home!

Darcey MacLennan (8)
Callander Primary School, Bridgend

Lola's Christmas Aventure

It's Christmas and I am in Mrs Claus' house and we're having tea. Then Santa said, "Why is this toy left behind? I must have forgotten to put it in my bag, probably because it was the dog's toy." Then Santa put me in a huge sack on his sleigh.
I said to the other toys, "Hi, my name is Lola." Suddenly, Santa slammed the brakes on and I fell out! There was another toy that fell out with me. We both held hands and we did somersaults as we tumbled through the sky, we landed in Dubai! Merry Christmas.

Sophie Corrieri (8)
Callander Primary School, Bridgend

Meleana's Big Adventure

It's Christmas Eve and all of the toys are getting packed in Santa's sleigh. In a sack is a doll. She has a red skirt, a green top and cute shoes. Her name is Meleana. Santa jumped on the sleigh. Suddenly, the sleigh came to a halt. Meleana fell out. She tumbled through the sky and landed in a jungle. Suddenly, something jumped down, it was a girl! She picked Meleana up and ran to her tree house. She told Meleana she was called Kelter. Santa had forgotten all about Meleana. Meleana stayed and they had Christmas dinner.

Katherine Lee (8)
Callander Primary School, Bridgend

Brown Bear's Christmas Journey

Hi, my name is Rose and I like paying tig. My friend is Mrs Claus because she is kind. I'm a bear and I'm brown and furry. Mrs Claus gave me a furry coat to keep warm. I put it on and sat beside Santa in his sleigh. Then the sleigh began to shake and everybody was scared. We fell out in London. We dropped under the Queen's tree. It had beautiful decorations, so much it was blinding me! It was morning and the Queen walked in. Everyone stopped and froze! The Queen looked at us and said, "Merry Christmas."

Michaela Lee (8)
Callander Primary School, Bridgend

What My Toys Do When I'm Not Home!

Hello there, my name is Wengie. I'm eight years old and it is the day before Christmas! But the day before this was awful as my owner shouted at me! Anyway, you're wondering what toy I am. I am an LPS! I have some friends, they are called Phoebe, Jake, Alison, Mike, Opal, Fruitie and finally, Angela. We did some naughty things like her room looked like World War 3 in there! My best friend was an ice cube with a snowflake inside but when I went to check on her she was gone! She had melted! Anyway, bye-bye.

Ula Czarnecka (8)
Callander Primary School, Bridgend

Swoop's Christmas Adventure!

I'm a toy owl and my name is Swoop. I'm getting wrapped and the elves are putting me into the sack. We're going to go around the world. Suddenly, I fell out of the sledge and fell through the chimney and landed in the Christmas tree! The Queen's Christmas tree! I had to abseil down the tinsel. I jumped off the tinsel and landed on the presents and then I jumped on the floor. I was walking down the hall and the Queen picked me up and I was scared, then she offered me a hot chocolate and marshmallows!

Euan Alexander Budge (8)

Callander Primary School, Bridgend

Plag's Amazing Adventure!

Hi, it's Christmas Eve today. My name is Plag. I'm four years old and it's time to get ready to go to London. It's so exciting because Santa is putting his presents on his sleigh. I held another toy's hand. We fell into Liberty of London. It was a cold night and my new friends and I walked into the carpet department and a nice lady said hello and gave us a cup of cocoa. It was fun, we got to sleep in the toy department.

The next day a little boy came and bought me. We had such fun!

Skye Reid (8)
Callander Primary School, Bridgend

Bouno Natale Beanie Boo!

It's Christmas Eve, 2017. Hi, my name is Bandit and I am a Beanie Boo. My favourite thing to do is play with my new owner. I was made in Santa's workshop. My owner is called Rosie, she's nine now but she still loves me. I saw a Christmas tree and climbed it. Santa almost saw me! Then I saw something rustling, I went to see what it was, it was a Rudolph toy! He spoke to me in Italian and I knew a bit. "Ciao Rudolph, cosa chi fi qi? Bouno Natale." We went to Nonna's for Christmas.

Kirsty Masters (8)
Callander Primary School, Bridgend

A Hungarian Christmas Adventure!

Hi, my name is Bandit and I'm a Beanie Boo. I will tell you a true story about me. Now let's go back to 2015 Christmas Eve, 24th December. I was flying with Santa and I fell out! I landed in a train station in Hungary! A boy picked me up. His name was Lazar, he took me to his house. He was bad. He chucked me around. There was a teddy called Bob. He had a plan, we escaped! We went to my granny's house and had a Christmas goulash and I heard Santa's bells ringing. "Ho, ho, ho!"

Oliver Brünner (8)
Callander Primary School, Bridgend

New York Christmas Adventure

Hello, my name is Epic and I'm a Lego man. I'm small and the elves are packing me into the sleigh. We have taken off! As we took off, oh I forgot to tell you, I was made in Santa's workshop. I'm going to peek out. Wow, it's amazing. It's all lit up. Down below it's New York! Suddenly, aah, no, I fell out of the sleigh. Ouch, that hurt! I looked around and I saw that I was on an island. The Statue of Liberty Island. Finally, I saw a red helicopter, it was... Mrs Claus.

Peter William McCleary (8)
Callander Primary School, Bridgend

Donny's Christmas Adventure!

Hello, I'm Donny and it is Christmas Eve. I'm a Ninja Turtle toy. Keira is asleep and I have heard a noise. I want to go and see what the noise is, the Christmas lights are on and I rode on the banister. When I opened the living room door I saw Geordie the dog who pounced up on me. Geordie was growling at me. So I swung on the Christmas stocking and I landed on the Christmas tree. The pine needles were so, so spiky! I threw a Christmas cookie and Geordie scoffed it up! Geordie fell asleep.

Keira Louise Little (7)
Callander Primary School, Bridgend

Zoomer's Christmas Adventure!

Hello, my name's Zoomer, you will love me! Here's a story about me. Let's go to Christmas Eve, 24th of December, when I was made. All the toys were nice, I would like to stay and play but I have to go to my new owner. The elves put me in a bag and put me in Santa's sleigh. I fell off Santa's sleigh with a toy called Zoe. We fell into a house in Holland! We fell in a Christmas tree! We got down the tree, the people were coming downstairs! We escaped. Santa came to get us!

Ailis Mercer McCluskey (8)
Callander Primary School, Bridgend

The Magic Island

Hey, I'm a Barbie called Lavender. I've got a dog called Lemons. I'm going to tell you the story of when I went to the magic island. I was sailing in the sea. Then all of a sudden, a hole burst in the boat and it began to sink! I fell overboard and Lemons too! I looked all around and saw an island. But I didn't know it was the magic island. So I decided to swim there and I found a magic grotto. It was beautiful and had sparkling waters. Then I appeared in my owner's house. Magic!

Naomi Grace Archibald (8)
Callander Primary School, Bridgend

Squeak's Wish Comes True!

It's Christmas Eve and my name is Squeak and I was made two years ago. I live in a fridge. However, that is fine with me because I'm a penguin! My wish for Christmas is to be out in open space but not in the warm, but in the cold. I would love to live in the North Pole. I hope it comes true. Suddenly, I heard a bang! It was coming from the chimney. I got out my bed and had a peek. I could see Santa! He said, "Come on Squeak, let's go," and *whoosh!* We were gone!

JJ Mcintyre (8)
Callander Primary School, Bridgend

Zoe's Christmas Adventure!

Hello, my name is Zoe and I'm a cute puppy toy. It's Christmas Eve and I'm getting delivered to my owner at a house in Callander, Mr Claus said. I got put in a box with a lovely red bow. Mr Claus was eating a sandwich when I fell out of the sleigh! I landed on the Christmas tree. There's a toy on the tree with me called Zoom. I saw him on the sleigh. The only thing is that she has two dogs that are very big! Santa rescued us, we were in a lovely red box, shhh! Dogs!

Keira Hindle (7)
Callander Primary School, Bridgend

Christmas At Smiggle's!

Hi, my name is Lily and I'm in Santa's house. Then I said hi to Mr and Mrs Claus. Then they gave me some mince pies. They were very good! Mr Claus and Mrs Claus were very nice to me and just then Santa said to me, "Come on Lily! Let's go for a ride in my sleigh."
I said, "Yes, I would like that." Suddenly, Santa stopped the sleigh. Then I fell out of the sleigh and I landed in the Smiggle's shop. It was fun using all of the pens.

Molly Hood (8)
Callander Primary School, Bridgend

Me And The Bear!

It's Christmas Eve and the elves had just finished making me. My name is Storm and I'm a reindeer. Suddenly, I was put in a box and then dropped into a sack. Then we started to move and I fell out of the sack. I fell down and down and down and I landed with a crunch. I gasped. I ran my hoof across the snow. Then I saw in the distance a cave, the bear from the John Lewis Christmas advert was just waking up to meet him at the Christmas Tree. Merry Christmas.

Maiya Gall (8)
Callander Primary School, Bridgend

The Best Day Ever!

It's Christmas Eve and my name is Keith and I'm in Africa. I am getting delivered to my new owner and I don't know his name yet. Wow! I was in the sleigh and I fell into a water park and then I saw another toy falling down a slide. He was cheering and I was just staring at him because he looked like a small Lego man! When I was in the park I saw a staircase leading to the water slide. I climbed and climbed and then jumped, it was amazing.

Liam Edmunds (9)
Callander Primary School, Bridgend

Pixy's Zoo Adventure

Hi, my name is Pixy and I am a Beanie Boo. It is Christmas Eve and I am in Santa's bag of toys as I'm getting a new owner. I hope he or she is nice and loves me and cares for me. Suddenly, I fall out of the sleigh. I landed in Glasgow Zoo! I saw big giraffes and one of them spotted me and it thought I was a leaf! So it chased me around! Then someone opened the door. Finally, I saw the sleigh, it was Santa and he took me to my owner. She was nice!

Brooke Cumming (8)
Callander Primary School, Bridgend

Storm The Remote-Controlled Car

Today it's Christmas Eve and my name is Storm. I'm a remote-control car and I'm in the North Pole. I'm in Santa's sack. I saw Santa's grotto and it was so cold. Suddenly, I fell out of Santa's sleigh into London and I went on to the London Eye. I saw Buckingham Palace and people skating under a big Christmas tree. Finally, Santa came back for me and I got to my house and I fell into the Christmas tree!

Alexander Brown (8)
Callander Primary School, Bridgend

Buster's Australian Adventure!

It's Christmas Eve and my name is Buster. I am about to get on Santa's sleigh. I am in a big sack, *whoosh*, and suddenly I was in the sky. Suddenly I tumbled out of the sleigh. My friend tumbled out too! Just then, I was in Australia. We saw the Statue of Red Dog in Dampier, We patted him on the head. Suddenly, Santa came back for me! He said, "So glad to find you, Buster! Merry Christmas!"

Archie Little (8)
Callander Primary School, Bridgend

Spider-Man Goes To Disneyland Paris!

It's Christmas Eve and my name is Spider-Man. I was made in Santa's workshop. I went to my new owner but I fell out of the sleigh over Disneyland, Paris. I fell on a bouncy castle and I went on some rides. It started to snow and I heard sleigh bells and Santa shouting, "Where are you Spider-Man?" "I'm here Santa, Merry Christmas."

Robbie McCorgray (8)
Callander Primary School, Bridgend

My Toy Story

"Let's get the walkie-talkies for the soldiers," said Bucky.
"And make sure Nick or his mom sees us," said Mary Potmeal.
"Right, he's... he's opening his last present," said the sergeant.
"But what has he got?" said Bucky.
"Oh, yeah... yes he's got an antiphobia man figure," said the sergeant. "Now it's his last present. It's the space ranger," said Sergeant.
"Oh what's this? Oh don't mind if I do," said Bucky.
"I hate you, we have been kidnapped," said Space Ranger.
"Okay, let's break out now," said Bucky.
"Let's be friends now."

Luca Richards (9)
Dalmellington Primary School, Dalmellington

Audrey's Pretend Fight

Once upon a time in a bedroom far away in Dalmellington, a boy named Thomas bought a teddy and named it Audrey. He went to bed with it, he played with it. But when he left... he came alive! "Hey there! I'm Audrey! Over here it's very light, but over there at Nad's team it's very dark," said Audrey. "Y'know we're having a fake wrestling match! We're planning for it. Before we start, I'll introduce you to my friends.

"Lucy."

"Hi."

"Jamie."

"Hi."

"Ellie."

"Hi!"

Before they could start Thomas stood on them! They all started to laugh!

Corey Denny (9)
Dalmellington Primary School, Dalmellington

Toy Story

Woody was a toy who lived in a bedroom. He came alive! He went out of the bedroom, there was a bed, desk and chest that says 'toys' and some books.
Five minutes later, he met a new friend that stays in the chest. "Hello," said Woody.
"Hello," said the friend.
"Let's go on an adventure."
First, in the bedroom, they went to the chest. "That is where I live." They went almost everywhere.
"We'll explore the rest tomorrow."
The next day they went to explore the rest of the castle.

Stephen Steele (9)
Dalmellington Primary School, Dalmellington

Minion Adventure

Once upon a time, there were toy Minions in Smyths Toy Store and every night they came to life. Every night they run about the store all night long. But one night they had a plan to escape to another store. Some other Minions disagreed about leaving Smyth's Toy Store and refused to leave. These Minions stayed at the Smyth's Toy Store while the other Minions left. The Minions came back with a sad face as the other stores were locked up and the Minions had to come home. The Minions went back to normal, running around the store.

Max Cumming (9)
Dalmellington Primary School, Dalmellington

The Dolphin

Every day a toy dolphin called Charlie and her family go for a quiet swim. Her parents tell her, "Don't go too far out." On the journey to the middle of the sea, she meets a seahorse called Larry. Then his twin comes along called Larry2. The twins go to an unknown place, but what Charlie doesn't know is that Larry2 is a bad one and when she realises it is too late! She gets sucked into a whirlpool.

After a year Charlie finally gets reunited with her family and has a massive shark as a pet.

Amber Grierson (9)
Dalmellington Primary School, Dalmellington

Bear's Journey

The teddy bear was new to the house. The teddy bear made friends easily, they made a plan to steal food, they were nearly there and were lucky not to be caught when going back upstairs.

While everyone was sleeping, the teddy bear and his friends were playing chase. The teddy bear was caught by the dog! He chased the bear all over the house. When he was caught the dog wanted to play, throwing the bear up in the air and shaking him. Then the bear's head fell off. The bear's owner sewed it back together.

Kevin Cullen (9)
Dalmellington Primary School, Dalmellington

One Great Adventure

In a little boy's room, there was a teddy called Ted. He didn't like adventures but he preferred to be played with. Ted's owner took all the toys out to play so they came to life. "Why don't you come on an adventure with us?" said one toy.
"No, no, I'll wait until our owner comes back," said Ted.
"Why don't you give it a try?" said one robot toy.
"Okay," said Ted.
Soon he tried it and he loved it. So he went on an adventure every day!

Billie-Jo Mullen (9)
Dalmellington Primary School, Dalmellington

The Adventure Of Sergeant Robot

Once upon a time, a toy was bought at Toys 'R' Us by a boy called Jake. The toy was called Sergeant Robot and he was taken home to be played with. He got home and Jake started to play with Sergeant Robot. Jake left for dinner, it was his time to escape! He ran out of the room into the hallway, dodging the ladders of the dark attic. He was in the kitchen dodging past all of the chairs. The next room was the living room, he entered there, he saw Jake's dad. Sergeant Robot glided and he escaped.

Ryan Stark (10)
Dalmellington Primary School, Dalmellington

The Boy That Loved Wrestling

Once upon a time, there was a little boy called Jamie. He loved wrestlers so he went to the wrestling shows all the time. He had a lot of wrestling toys but he wanted more so he went and bought some on Saturday afternoon. But they weren't just any wrestlers, they were alive! The boy bought them thinking they were normal toys but when he went away they moved, so whenever he got back he was very confused because he left them on the floor, but they were always in the ring and they became friends.

Eilidh Chapman (9)
Dalmellington Primary School, Dalmellington

Spirit's Adventure

Once there was a toy horse called Spirit. He's a great jumper when he comes alive, with his owner and him soaring high over the logs and cross poles. The human's name is Mia, she is ten.
His owner got him for Christmas with a jumping ring, also tacks and a stable. His owner is smart and intelligent. Spirit is a pro at show jumping. They were on holiday, they were in Spain. They have been down to the beach and they love Spain!

Kaidi McLurkin (10)
Dalmellington Primary School, Dalmellington

Ted's Adventure

At first, Ted was in a massive shop. When he was in the shop every friend of his was getting picked but him, but finally, he got picked. When the owners took him he didn't feel the best because it's his first time in a house and there was a dog chasing him. A weird boy came in and was playing with him with other teddies and his other brother came in and stared at him and the boy joined in with his brother and started to join in with him and Ted and the dog.

Daylon Fawcett (9)
Dalmellington Primary School, Dalmellington

The Ball

Once upon a time, 100 toy Minions were in a car going to a ball. There was a prince Minion waiting for a wife. The boy and girl Minions all arrived at the ball. There was food and drinks, all were happy having fun at the ball. The clock at the ball was made out of gold! All the things that you could see were all gold.
After ten hours all the Minions went to the bed. The Minions got a fright as a dark shadow appeared and it really scared them.

Aiden Milligan (9)
Dalmellington Primary School, Dalmellington

Hulk And His Evil Twin

Once there was a toy named the Hulk but his team got infected by his evil brother and they are trying to kill him but he is the strongest toy in the world. Then they came one by one, they all went down and they turned back to normal. They found the evil Hulk so they tried to knock him out, but he was too strong so they lured him into a trap that is in a toy box so they let him chase the Hulk into the toy box. The Hulk gets out, they win.

Matthew Wilson (10)
Dalmellington Primary School, Dalmellington

Tedster's Life

Tedster was in a shop with other teddies. All the teddies were waiting to be bought, then Tedster's best friend was bought. Then eight other teddies came in. Then Tedster made a new best friend and his name was Buttons. His last owner left him, then two days passed and Tedster was bought with his new best friend.

Dylan Murphy (9)
Dalmellington Primary School, Dalmellington

The Truth

The teddy bear glided off the shelf and was greeted by his friends. But he was not acting like himself. He was bumping into his friends and the furniture. "What's up?" said his best friend, the unicorn.

"Nothing," said Teddy.

"Just tell me what's up."

"I told you, it's nothing," the teddy bear shouted. As he turned around he bumped into the bed and his leg came flying off. The toys came running up with his leg.

"Tell us what's wrong," said the unicorn.

"I can't see."

"Well, it's nothing to be ashamed of. We will take you to Specsavers."

Lucie Reid (10)
Danderhall Primary School, Danderhall

Dino Disaster

Rex was swinging around like a monkey. *Ripp!* The curtains tore. Rex came plummeting down. He hit the bed, bounced up and flew out the window. *Crash!* His tail fell off. *Roar!* The toys heard him and warned the army men. They marched into the bathroom, formed a human pyramid and grabbed the toilet paper. Buzz held one end while they abseiled down to save Rex. Mr Potato Head looked around for something. "Aha!" He found sticky gum and stuck his tail back on. "*Roar*, that hurt, but thanks Doc!" The toys rushed into the box when Tony came. "Night."

Kaitlyn Munro (10)
Danderhall Primary School, Danderhall

Untitled

The teddy tried to wriggle out of something but didn't know what. He tried harder and harder then fell, but he somehow felt lighter. After a while of worrying, he looked down and screamed, "Aaaahhh."
Suddenly, the toys came out of their positions and looked up and yelled, "It's a dog."
"With my feet," the teddy added. The dog slobbered all over his feet whilst biting into it with a playful manner. But eventually, the dog spat the teddy's feet out and the teddy got sewed back together and he looked as good as new like he'd never been sewn.

Leo Wilson (10)
Danderhall Primary School, Danderhall

The Baby

A long time ago, a baby doll was sent to Toys 'R' Us. Whenever people came no one wanted to buy her.

Years went past, she was getting older so one day someone put her up in the attic. Days, weeks, months went past. She got angrier and angrier. One day she made a plan to destroy the new toys so she could be the only one left. That's what happened. Everyone was in their boxes, she started with the action figures, then the stuffed animals, lastly the dolls. Every toy was gone.

The next day, the toys were back!

Maia Makorie (10)
Danderhall Primary School, Danderhall

Trouble!

Buzz was charging on the shelf when there was a scream. He got in a tizzy and unplugged himself. He jumped down off the shelf and ran downstairs and there was another scream louder than before. Buzz was really scared, then the danger came. Pink Violet jumped out with a knife and Buzz ran upstairs and phoned the police. He realised that the scream was fake. Suddenly, Pink Violet chased him. The police came and Pink Violet was getting told off by the police and then they became friends. She is a nice person now, not mean.

Emma Kennedy (10)
Danderhall Primary School, Danderhall

Woody And Rex's Revenge

The eight-legged robotic baby ran like the wind to the front door desperately trying to escape. But just then, Woody and Rex caught Spider Baby and put him in a cage. Rex roared so loud that Spider Baby's face turned inside out. It was horrific! He realised this was revenge for taking their best friend. So he slumped down in a corner of the cage. Woody and Rex were tired so they went to sleep.

In the morning, they noticed Spider Baby was gone and so was the cage! A trail led to the cupboard under the stairs...

Cameron Sean Peter Elliot (10)
Danderhall Primary School, Danderhall

Slynkie's Night-Time Adventure

One full moon Cessie tidied her room and went to bed. Slynkie was the only one awake. He couldn't get to sleep so he decided he would explore parts of the house he had never been to before. He was a little bit hungry, so he went to the place the humans called the kitchen but Slynkie was going to call it Foodland. So off Slynkie went to get food. He ate a burger, a pizza, a strawberry ice cream and finally, he went back to bed. Thankfully, Cessie didn't wake up and Slynkie fell asleep in his cosy bed.

Cassie Shaw (10)
Danderhall Primary School, Danderhall

The War Between Bad And Good

The bad toys started hurting everyone in the room. The toy soldiers heard all the commotion, got their guns and came out. The toys saw the soldiers. The toy soldiers started shooting and they all died apart from one. It saw it was all alone so it went to hide. The soldiers stayed where they were. The bad toy started to sneak up on them very slowly because he didn't want to die. But there was still a toy called Rex (he is quite clumsy though). He jumped off the shelf and landed and killed the toy.

Taylor Russell (10)
Danderhall Primary School, Danderhall

Untitled

"Hey, wake up, wake up."

"What? Who are you?"

"I'm Bridget, I only have enough time here so we better act fast."

"Act fast on what?"

"Act fast on getting out of here."

"Why?" said Violet.

Bridget said, "Because Carla never plays with us, we're nothing to her."

"Carla loves us so much."

"Are you sure about that?"

"Yes," said Violet.

"Well then, when was the last time she played with you?"

"Five months ago."

"Well then, are you in?"

"I'm in," said Violet.

"Let's get started."

"How are we going to do this?" said Violet.

"Just wait and see..."

Emilie Thomson (10)
Kirkliston Primary School, Kirkliston

Marksman Spotters

There was Ollie, he was a little drone, and there was Private Ryan, he owned the army marksman spotters. There were another five of us including Mr Sergeant Peters and they had two flying drones, Black Eye and Red Eye. They were dangerous.

"Leo, get up, it's time for school."

"Alright, I'm getting up, right I'm ready."

"Have you brushed your teeth?"

"Aww no, I forgot."

"Quick, go do them OK?"

"Did you just move my toys?"

"No why?"

"Because my room's trashed and the bathroom is as well."

"Who cares, you'll be late."

..."Jeez, that was a close one."

Leo Evans (9)
Kirkliston Primary School, Kirkliston

Toy Mayhem

It started in Sammy's bedroom at 7.45am. Sammy was snoozing in bed, suddenly his toy circles crawled off the shelf.

"Hello, I'm Jolly Jessie. These are my friends Grumpy Gregor, Nerdy Noah, Clumsy Chloe and Mischievous Molly."

"We're trying to escape this prison cell," said Chloe.

"It's called a bedroom," said Noah.

"Come on, let's go," said Gregor.

"According to my calculations, we have five minutes until the human's time circle erupts," said Noah.

"QUICK!" The five toy circles dashed across the room. Sammy woke up and saw his toys lying on the bedroom floor!

"What a mess!" Sammy sighed.

Siya Ramsohok (10)
Kirkliston Primary School, Kirkliston

Adventurous Jenny The Unicorn

"Ouch!" said the scabby lion, bouncing back like a ball.

"Keep pulling," howled the claustrophobic, grumpy unicorn.

"Why are we doing this?" cried the weepy emoji.

"Because I ain't being stuck in this ridiculous box. Yes, I am free, I can go anywhere. Move out of my way peasants," said the unicorn, whilst confidently wandering out.

"Wait! Before you leave, how do you get your fur to be pink, fluffy and marshmallow-like?"

"What?" spoke the confused unicorn.

"I said..."

"Aaah! What was that? It looks like Lucy, run."

"She's gonna squish us," said Squishy...

Lucy Elder (10)
Kirkliston Primary School, Kirkliston

Energy... Away!

"Hey!" whispered Violei, "Sofia's gone. Wake up you guys, wake up." There was silence for a moment. "Why aren't you waking up? Come on guys, stop messing around..."
"Well hello there Violei!" Violei jumped. "Don't be scared Violei. Just look up."
Violei cautiously looked up and saw a pink toy raccoon. "Well, Violei, I don't have much time, but I am Roxie, and I took your friend's energy away! Okay, bye-bye," and off she disappeared.
"Zeesh!" exclaimed Violei. "Anyway, I know where the holy powers are hidden, so I can just go and get them."
But then Mum came in...

Sofia Robb (10)
Kirkliston Primary School, Kirkliston

Meka And Teka's Adventure

"Oh, hi, my name's Meka."
"My name's Teka."
"We are best friends."
Meka is a giraffe and Teka is a lion.
"We are on a mission."
Emma is having a donation at her school. Sadly she has donated Barbie, Woof Woof and Barney.
"We need to go to the garage and save them before they go to school."
"Well, what are we waiting for, let's go."
"Yeah!" They went downstairs to the garage. There they were, sitting in a box saying 'donation'.
"Let's get them." They got the box and took it upstairs back in Emma's bedroom. "We got them!"

Sophie Stewart (9)
Kirkliston Primary School, Kirkliston

Pomm With The Escape

"Before this, I was loved by a magnificent owner, we went everywhere together. But now I am stuck in this stuffy, elderly grabber machine," complained Pomm.
"Why don't you escape?" asked Suki.
"You know, that's not a bad idea!"
"Right, I am as ready as ever," Pomm said. She approached the exit of the machine, with all the toys staring anxiously.
"Stop!" shouted Suki in fear. "A gigantic girl is coming, everybody go hide!" Suddenly, there was a clacking noise, then, the dusty stiff grabber started to move closer and closer until it stopped in front of Pomm...

Lanah Banks (10)
Kirkliston Primary School, Kirkliston

Untitled

Once upon a time... "Let's go! Let's get out of here," said a golden, furry, big-eyed bear, "let's get out." They got out of an open window. Lightning hitting, it set fire to a wood store, next to the wood store was a park. "Oh no, aaah," Brody, the bear, sighed. "Let's get in," said Brody. They got back in. The car came back picking Jim from the school run. They hid.

"Get away from my spot," said Dave. Brody punched him in the face.

Jim came in, "What the heck?" said Jim.

"Um, it's not what you think."

"Run!"

Aaron Michael McVeigh (10)
Kirkliston Primary School, Kirkliston

Playroom Derby

Greg's alarm goes. He leaves for school.
Downstairs the greatest fixture is starting, Blues vs
Reds. Formation for today's fixture, Reds, 4, 4, 2,
Blues, 4, 3, 3. The referee's whistle blasts off.
Number 3 for Reds starts the match. He kicks it to
number 7. He dribbles and cuts inside. He hits the
bar! It falls to number 4. He hits it bottom left. 1-0
to Reds.
Blues attack. Number 10 hits it into the box. 6
headers it. 1-1. The door opens. It's Greg. He looks
suspicious and wonders why his players scattered
all around his bedroom floor.

Gregor Burn (10)
Kirkliston Primary School, Kirkliston

Save The Poos

It was night-time and everyone was asleep, except for Babyjeffkins. He was my scented poo emoji. "Ha, ha. ha, I am Babyjeffkins and I am going to make this house smell like poo by building an army of poos, I just did some right now and it was nice. Someone is coming, I should hide before they kill me..."

Poo down!

"I need to save them by making more."

The smell was getting stronger, the humans were making plans and Babyjeffkins was making poo. Soon the humans were gone.

"Let's celebrate and have a slumber party! War is over, poops."

Yoshua Mthokozisi Gordon (10)
Kirkliston Primary School, Kirkliston

The Death Of The Unbeatable

Jumping off the shelf and gliding through the air like a perfect glider, landing on the bed with a thud, all the other toys scattering from the misunderstood Rubix. The closest gun was a measly pistol. "Minions, grab that gun, it'll help!" ordered the Rubix.

Creeping along the lounge floor, extremely isolated, Kuby and two of his minions were knocked by a Hoover. "Run!" bellowed the sergeant.

Kuby, his eyes open just enough to see a hand reaching down to grab him. "No," whispered the sergeant. The hand was icy-cold, but the bin was somehow worse than that!

Tom Ellaway (10)
Kirkliston Primary School, Kirkliston

Untitled

It was Monday morning and I had to go to school. "Okay, let's go," said the gang leader, so they snuck downstairs and got some food. They snuck back up and had a loud party. Crumbs everywhere. But things went a little bit too far, they snuck into my brother's room and messed it all up. Then went back into the room. Suddenly, the door slowly opened, "Positions!" shouted Doggy. But when my brother walked in, he blamed me!
"Wait a minute," I said.
"There's crumbs all over the floor."
"Oh no," whispered Piggy Power...

Abigail Beth Mclean (9)
Kirkliston Primary School, Kirkliston

The Battle Of Toys

One dark day the shadow car was zooming around when suddenly, there was a bullet heading right for him. He quickly dodged it. It was the Shadow's worst enemy, Mr Tiny! He was a tiny bear. "Hi there Shadow, were you looking for me?"
"Of course, this means war!" Shadow fired his machine gun but it missed because Mr Tiny was tiny. Mr Tiny unleashed his robots but Shadow shot them with his cap gun, Shadow was shooting his missiles next. Shadow shot and missed Mr Tiny. But here comes another. Suddenly, they stopped in the middle of the battle...

Albert Sienko (10)
Kirkliston Primary School, Kirkliston

Untitled

"OK, do you remember the plan?" said Rainbow the unicorn.

"Yes I do, we jump onto the bed and climb onto the windowsill and escape to Toys 'R' Us," said Hamish the Westie.

"Let's go," shouted Rainbow!" But suddenly, they heard a thump and then another thump, so they scurried back to the bed.

"I think it is Rose, the human," whispered Hamish. Slowly the door opened and as Rose walked in, "I don't remember putting my plushies on my bed; oh well, they are fine where they are."

Grace Ann Shedden (10)
Kirkliston Primary School, Kirkliston

The Day Of The Living Doll

One ordinary day, a girl called Lulu was getting ready for school, but something strange was going on. Lulu's doll Jess had moved from the bed to the bookshelf. "I will see if she will move when I get home," said Lulu.

"Lulu, are you ready? Your father is waiting in the car," called her mother. Off Lulu went, away to school.

"Is she gone?" Jess wondered. "Phew." Now that Lulu was away Jess got to work. She pulled out bins of toys and shoes and took the bedding off. Seven hours later Lulu got home...

Kara Mcneill (10)
Kirkliston Primary School, Kirkliston

Untitled

One day a toy cub was doing his ordinary dance routine when suddenly he saw a game, it was like an iPad, the disc was huge.

He pulled out his watch from his dark pocket and with a bang, a holograph showed up. "Hello Sergeant Hunter, you called?" said Sir Wigalot.

"Yes, I have found an unusual object, allowed to check it out?"

"Yes," shouted Sir Wigalot.

"It appears to be a game, over and out," said Hunter.

The cub galloped pretending to be a horse when he pulled to the game and put the game in...

Lucy Mclellan (10)
Kirkliston Primary School, Kirkliston

The Quest

As the door slams shut a rustling sound comes from the teddy box. Every teddy scrambles out including Fosy. Today Fosy decides to go on a quest to get to the Xbox, however, he needs to cross the dreaded, war-filled Lego World. Then Fosy hears a bang, he knows he's near to no-man's-land. Behind him, he sees the giant, dreaded cat-monkey.
Fosy has to run so he decided to sprint into no-man's-land, Fosy hears gunfire from both sides, then he sees the Xbox and jumps onto the chair and smashes down on the controller to play FIFA 18.

Ben Sansom (10)
Kirkliston Primary School, Kirkliston

Mr Kinklewink's Diary

Day 1

No one wants me here. I'm just an old, boring one-eyed toy frog. Timmy used to love me, now I'm all alone, abandoned in this ancient ship.

Day 2

Suddenly I woke up, and light filled the ship. The cool spring air brushed against my wrinkled face. Surprisingly, a huge hand reached out and grabbed me. What was going to happen?

Day 3

I got sold to a lovely owner who plays with me lots! And in the future, I'll keep getting passed on to other beautiful children. I might even come to you.

Scarlett McGuire (10)
Kirkliston Primary School, Kirkliston

Tragedy On The Stairs

"Okay, now is my chance!" murmured Corrie the toy fox as she scrambled across from the living room to the stairs. Suddenly, Corrie started clambering up the stairs but a pattering noise reached her...

Leaping out of nowhere, a fierce cat caught Corrie's tail! "No! I guess I was too overzealous..." suggested poor Corrie.

Rapidly thinking, Corrie's brain wasn't functioning properly. She had so many worries about the fearsome cat. Just as Yasmin came in, Corrie forgot about all the stress and relaxed.

Yasmin Mutiara Hunter (10)
Kirkliston Primary School, Kirkliston

The Day Of The Soldiers

One day James went out to celebrate his fantastic birthday, so this was the perfect time for the toy soldiers to do their assault on the teddy bear. Despite the size difference, the soldiers rambled on although they didn't have long until excited James came, so they cracked on. "Right, let's go boys!" soldier Dave said.

"Dave, James is going to be home soon, so let's hurry up and finish this assault!" soldier Fred said. Also, the bear was tired of defending himself, so he surrendered and that was it...

Fraser Innes Mitchell (10)
Kirkliston Primary School, Kirkliston

The Foxy And Mangle Story

One day I was starting my morning like any other. I was walking around the room, then suddenly I saw eyes peering out of Pirate's Cove. Are these the eyes of a new toy? I suddenly rushed over, there was a little fox curled up on one side. "It's okay, my name is Mangle, what's yours?"
"F-f-foxy."
I saw a glimpse of his sharp hook. "So you're a pirate?"
Foxy nodded, "Oh, you saw my hook?"
After a few hours, we were best friends, and a few days after we went on many adventures.

Morgan Middleton (10)

Kirkliston Primary School, Kirkliston

Untitled

"Hello, my name is Amina and I am a doll. Everyone loves me!" Well it's just a beautiful day and I am wanting to go and play in the garden. So I think I should go to the amazing garden. "Ow, what happened? Something just hit me!" I think it's just my imagination. Oh I can see a skipping rope, let's just go and get it. Just as I touch the rope there was a dog chasing me. "Oh help, I need help."

Then the dog says, "Hey, you have got my delicious bone." Then I gave him the bone.

Aamna Mahmood (10)
Kirkliston Primary School, Kirkliston

The Mission Of The Teddy Bears

"Psss Pudsey, Jessica's asleep, quick, let's go and find the chocolate brownie." We scrambled downstairs into the kitchen.

"Oh no, grr, look over there on the kitchen table, the chocolate brownie tin! Now to get past Spencer."

"Quickly, run over to that chair and climb up, watch out for the dog though."

"Phew, we made it, let's get stuck in. It's so yummy!"

But what they didn't realise was that they had made such a big mess! What was Jessica going to think...?

Alice Reedie (9)
Kirkliston Primary School, Kirkliston

The Moving Toys

It was a bright morning in a magical room full of toys, especially stuffed toy elephants, owned by a beautiful girl named Eilidh who was ten. One of the elephants, called Emilie, was on a mission to find her brother who had been across the room and into a toy box, where all the forgotten toys go. Emilie was not quite sure about how she would get there so she made a plan to cross the glass desk, catch the remote-control aeroplane from on the stool and simply jump onto the huge box; but how would she do that?

Carla Vaughan (10)
Kirkliston Primary School, Kirkliston

Untitled

Out in the atmosphere, a shady black figure of a toy stumbled towards me with his bright red devil eyes, I felt terrified with shivers running down my spine. Suddenly, I saw two massive sharp crab claws, it also had this worm-looking thing on his head. He also had a gigantic, outspoken mask. But he had colourful red teeth like he had been drinking blood. Suddenly, he stumbled towards me, he stopped. This black figure was six foot tall, then he said, "My name is Toby," in a low voice. We fought till the sun went up, I won.

Rebecca Thorington (10)
Kirkliston Primary School, Kirkliston

Untitled

As the dog woke up, it heard a strange noise coming from under the bed. The toy dog pricked its ears as the sound came again. *Scratch, scratch, scratch.* The dog slowly got out of his bed and crept towards the door.

He opened it. Then he ran to the top of the stairs and jumped. Then he ran across the corridor to find his owner and told him what he'd heard upstairs.

So the owner slowly went upstairs and reached the room. Then he crawled under the bed and heard a purring sound and saw... a little, furry kitten.

Wang Sum Lo (10)
Kirkliston Primary School, Kirkliston

Bears On A Mission

"Shh, keep the noise down," whispered Bear One. So the four bears kept on moving forward to the lounge where the TV was on. They scanned the area but it wasn't clear their owner was walking towards them, Bear Two yelled, "Run." But Bear Four didn't make it, he got kicked and went flying across the room, the three others didn't have time to save him and they just made it through the door to the kitchen. In the kitchen it is another level, it is way harder to survive. There was a house party...

Blair Roberts (10)
Kirkliston Primary School, Kirkliston

Help Me!

Gregor came back from school, he had his dinner, he ran to his room. He was going to watch TV until he noticed one of his favourite teddies. Gregor went to grab him but he heard a sound like, "Help me." He got scared so he ran to the toilet.

When he came back the teddy was gone, now he's in the basketball hoop with the basketball in his mouth. He grabbed him and said, "Why is this happening?" Then a bag dropped on his head. Gregor took the bag off and his least favourite teddy was standing there.

Evan Ross (10)
Kirkliston Primary School, Kirkliston

Lance's Super Mech Gets Stolen!

Once there was a toy knight called Lance. Now Lance originally didn't always want to be a knight, he wanted to be an actor, but then his parents sent him to knight school. There he met his future knightly friends: Clay, Macey, Aroon and Axl.

So you join in the middle of a battle between the Nexo Knights and the evil minions of Jestro and the book of monsters. It looks like the Nexo knights are in trouble. Lance's super mech is failing.

Clay, Macey and Axl are fighting hard but could it be too late?...

Andrew Kerr (10)
Kirkliston Primary School, Kirkliston

The Night Of The Rabbit

"I think Tommy's asleep," said Spencer. "I think I'll look around." Spencer looked around everywhere but could not find anyone, so he went into the kitchen to see the thing he adored so much. A carrot. He tried climbing to get the carrot but his paws could not climb up the wall. He got an idea. "I'll grab that toy plane Tommy got." After hopping in the plane he went to the stairs, drove off and flew but as soon as he tried he crashed with a bang. Tommy awoke, he picked up Spencer...

Cameron Proudfoot (10)
Kirkliston Primary School, Kirkliston

Rolly

It was a cold, magical Christmas Eve. The little toy was all by himself in the toy store. No one had taken him home. He jumped off the shelf and rolled over the smooth floor and looked out the misty window with his teary eye, but at that very moment, he saw a shooting star and wished to be someone's special toy.

Santa came up to the window and opened the creaky door and said, "Ho, ho, ho, I have just the home for you." So the toy jumped on the sleigh and up they went to his special home!

Lucy Richmond (10)
Kirkliston Primary School, Kirkliston

Untitled

Once, there was a little puppy toy that lives under my bed (when I'm not playing with it). While I was away, Mister Lance came out from under my bed, then let out a few barks to make sure I wasn't there. As you know I wasn't there... so he went on an adventure around the room.

Then he sees my clothes... and he walks over. Then I walk in, seeing him trying to rip up my clothes. But he is a toy, he has no teeth! So I wasn't angry, but I was puzzled at how he got there.

Jamie Josh Sinclair (10)
Kirkliston Primary School, Kirkliston

The Cheeky Bear Day

One day, I left for school at 8.25am as usual and without me knowing, upstairs in the bedroom mischief was going on. The silly, cheeky bear Spencer sneaked some sour candy out of the locked jar into the cupboard and put them on a plate and put some in the blender with some apple juice and made an unhealthy smoothie for himself! Then when he went back into bed with his snack he got his iPad out and put YouTube on and started watching slime videos. Once he had finished he made slime. That bear!

Ruby Corson (10)
Kirkliston Primary School, Kirkliston

The Day Of The Living Unicorns

One day a little girl called Maya was playing with her two favourite unicorns called Candyfloss and Rainbowfloss, and they are on a mission to go somewhere once Maya was away at school.
"Maya, it's time to go to school now."
"Okay Mum, coming. Bye Candyfloss and Rainbowfloss."
"Let's go now."
"Okay Candyfloss, let's go."
Then they leapt around the room to get their silver crowns before Maya came back from school.

Brooke Thomson (10)
Kirkliston Primary School, Kirkliston

The Crazy World Of Spot's Bedroom

As the sun sinks over the horizon, the little boy fell asleep. Spot the toy dog ran around the bedroom and started to bark as loud as a lion and the little boy started to wiggle in his bed. Then all the toys started to surround Spot. He was terrified, then the toys came closer and closer. Then Spot panicked and pushed some toys out of the way. He ran as fast as he could. All the toys were chasing him, then Spot realised that the toys would never do this to him, they were his best friends.

Léa Hogg (10)
Kirkliston Primary School, Kirkliston

Dan The Half-Tailed Dinosaur

Crash, bang, smash! It was a dinosaur, but it wasn't any old toy dinosaur. He had half a tail and his name was Dan. Annoyingly, when Sam slammed his bedroom door shut that caused Dan to wake up. But before you knew it, he was riding on Sam's favourite toy truck. And then the toy army arrived, so first they tried to take Dan down, but that didn't work. Then something started to fall out of the sky. It was half of a tail. Dan caught it and then he just vanished!

Lewis Robert Alexander Briggs (10)
Kirkliston Primary School, Kirkliston

The Race

Upon the horizon of the bedroom light, the R8 posed, just lingering for a race. It waits and waits, then an Aventador rolls up. It challenges the R8, it accepts. They line up, the light changes, they are off. The R8 is winning until the battery runs out. The Aventador wins as the R8 gets towed away, it is the most hated car in the room. The R8 trains all night, then it was ready, they both line up, the light turns green and the race was on, *vroom*...

Calum Russell Gilmore (10)
Kirkliston Primary School, Kirkliston

Untitled

"Okay!" said a small thing, it was Pikachu, it was a small, yellow, cute Pokémon.

"But anyway, now you can go to Ben's house," said a pink pig plushie toy. Pikachu and Pig were just about to go on a Pokébattle . "Maybe we can use the tunnel that we dug last time?"

One hour later, they were in Ben's house, but before they could start, Teddy shouted, "Ben is back from school..."

Tymek Rusinek (10)
Kirkliston Primary School, Kirkliston

The Mission Of The Dogs

One Thursday afternoon, two teddies were living on the bed. Their names are Patch and Fudge, Fudge has long, messy hair and Patch has short, soft hair. Patch was the mischievous, curious one and Fudge the goody-two-shoes.
They stood up and walked around trying to wake the others. Once everybody was awake they started getting up to mischief. Suddenly, the door swung open. "Uh-oh! Here comes Ella! She's home!"

Ella Rutherford (9)
Kirkliston Primary School, Kirkliston

Toys That Move

One beautiful day as I left for school, Bob and Jeff, my two twin teddies, ran down to the kitchen, Bob threw ice cream at Jeff. Jeff got really angry. Bob is laughing so much, he burped. Bob stopped laughing and got tomatoes and threw them at Jeff. Bob and Jeff got cream and put it on the walls. Bob heard the car zoom in, they ran up the stairs and sat on the bed with cream on their faces...

Thomas Kenneth Newport (10)
Kirkliston Primary School, Kirkliston

A Band Of Royals

One day, Princess Celestia was walking outside, she found a poster which said, 'Listen up rockers, we are hosting a battle of the bands. If you win, you get tickets to your favourite concert. What are you waiting for? Start now'. Celestia ran home as fast as she could. She got home and said, "Let's form a band."

"Okay," said Princess Twilight Sparkle, "but as long as I get to be lead singer."

Celestia shook her head and replied, "No, I'm lead singer."

They had a singing competition. They could be heard singing songs on the way upstairs all day!

Corrina Amy Joan Hood (10)

Langlands Primary School, Forfar

The Vicious Barbie

"Huh, what do you want you weirdos?" bellowed Loxi. "Aaahh, help! If you're going to sling me in a box then do it carefully," Loxi shouted at the top of her voice. Nobody heard her so she was tossed in roughly. Loxi started having a rummage about in the box. She found her enemy. "Hey, dumbo doolally idiot, get over here," commanded Loxi to her enemy, Daisy. Daisy had long straight hair and was very petite. "Let's have a fight," Loxi said to Daisy. Daisy wasn't very keen on having a fight but she took the challenge on.
"Let's go..."

Jodi Balfour (9)
Langlands Primary School, Forfar

The Wild School

A girl named Kate bought a new toy. It was a rabbit, she called it Floral. Kate brought the fuzzy, snow-white rabbit to school. The teacher, Miss Stewart, was not happy. She put the rabbit in the cupboard with the rest of the toys. But the rabbit talked, it said, "Oh no, it's dark in here." But the dragon said, "Wait, who's in here?"
"I'm Floral, I'm new here."
The dragon said, "Oh okay..."
Floral got taken out by the teacher and she gave her back to Kate. Kate went home with Floral and was as happy as anything.

Michaela Hart (8)
Langlands Primary School, Forfar

The Fighting Minions

Once upon a time, there was a plump, cute, yellow Minion who was a captain of one Minion team called the Winning 22. Their captain was called St Nickolis.

"What is happening Captain?" said Dave, who is the other Minion.

"We are about to battle the vicious 22." The battle began and a horn blew. *Bang. Bang.* Guns shot and made deafening banging noises. Finally, one Minion left and went to ride one of Tom's toy trains.

The battle ended a month later and the Minions were still extremely mad at each other. Finally, they forgot all about it.

Eilidh Bisset (9)

Langlands Primary School, Forfar

The Crazy Toys

We were in the car and on our way to camp in Skye. Meanwhile, back at home, the toys came out of the cupboards. The toy panda said, "Okay, everyone, let's calm down, let's see where the girl is."

Then one toy said, "Let's make the room like it's Halloween." They started trashing the place like mad! They were clapping hands and singing songs to each other. Everyone went down the stairs and into the cupboard of the bowls and plates, they damaged all of them.

When I got home everything was damaged, I was in shock, "What has happened?"

Sophia Cameron (9)
Langlands Primary School, Forfar

Eilianna Goes Missing!

Once there was a happy, excitable little girl called Melissa and she went shopping and got a rare multicoloured doughnut teddy. Melissa called her Eilianna. Melissa never knew toys came alive at night, but she knew they moved in the night.

The next day, Melissa hugged into Eilianna and her mum shouted, "Time to get your breakfast." And Melissa put Eilianna down next to a window and the wind picked up and blew Eilianna out of the window on to the ground. A few seconds later, Melissa went outside to pick her up but someone had taken her far away.

Willow Forrester (9)
Langlands Primary School, Forfar

The Friendship Toy Box

Once, a girl had a toy called Cali. She loved her so much she slept with her, but on her birthday she accidentally left Cali in the toy box. "Oh no," said Cali, everyone said that the toy box is dark and scary but it wasn't. There was a light in the toy box. She heard a voice, "Is anyone there?" She heard it again, she found a teddy cat. "Do you need help?"
"Yes please." They looked around and found another toy. It was a dog teddy called Paw. "Let's go," they shouted. They tried to get out.

Rebecca Anne Rebel Whitton (9)
Langlands Primary School, Forfar

The Magical Ty

Hi, I'm a Ty tiger. I live with a kind little girl called Mia, my name's Tiggs. When everybody is away I like to sneak out of the bedroom and have adventures. All the other toys say not to because it's dangerous, but I do it anyway. I tell them how fun it is. I have to wait till Mia's family go before my adventure starts but something wasn't right. Someone came in the house and stole me. Oh no! I want to escape. I'll wait till they're sleeping. I waited... thankfully, a window was open. I escaped. Never again!

Sophie Baikie (9)
Langlands Primary School, Forfar

Where Did He Go?

One sunny morning, Paul was eating breakfast in his bedroom, the toys were running around! But one toy was very quiet, his name was Squidgy Snake. He was Paul's favourite toy. Paul went back to his room and saw Squidgy Snake was in the wrong place. Paul left the room and counted to five, when he saw that Squidgy was gone! Paul was very sad, he looked everywhere and even the next day Squidgy didn't appear. Paul's mum said, "It's the quiz show." When they got there, guess who was sitting next to them? Squidgy Snake!

Paul de Veres (9)
Langlands Primary School, Forfar

Cheeky Little Hatchimals

One day, I was playing with my Hatchimal, Paws, then I had to go to school. When I left he went to go to get his friend, Waddles and went to find something to do. They found some balls and played with them for a while, passing them and throwing them. Paws' ball was adorable. Waddles' ball had miniature paw prints and Paws had butterflies, flowers and bees.

After playing with them for a while, they got tedious and went to find some rope. They found some really colossal rope and abseiled down my bed. I was so shocked.

Bethany Young (10)

Langlands Primary School, Forfar

Stuck In A House

There was a box in the middle of the forest. There were toys inside it. A child went and looked in the box. She took a toy out, it was a unicorn. The unicorn was real but she didn't know. She took the toy home and she played with it. The unicorn said, "I am going to escape." She flew under the bed, then the child came and she saw that the unicorn magically disappeared. The child was furious. She looked, she spotted the unicorn was sad so she decided to pull a funny face. Suddenly, the unicorn laughed hysterically.

Maja Stokes (9)
Langlands Primary School, Forfar

Miss Swish Grape Escapes

One day in class Abbi brought in her toy that was called Miss Swish Grape because it was show and tell. Miss Swish Grape got lost that day and Abbi couldn't find her anywhere. Abbi was very sad and upset. She heard a voice that said, "Don't be upset."

Abbi said, "Why? I've lost my new toy," and then she found out why she couldn't find Miss Swish Grape. She had escaped out of Abbi's bag and had gone home. She was tired and went to bed and she said, "Bye for now."

Abbi Ewen (8)

Langlands Primary School, Forfar

The Toys Are Up To Mischief

In the bedroom was an alien called Luke, two bees called Steven and Josh and a bear called Brooke. They were waiting for Rhys to leave so they could start their mission. When Rhys left, they climbed out of the bag. Brooke growled and the toys woke up. They wrecked his room!
When Rhys got back his room was a tip. He tidied it up, it took two hours. He went for a drink and when he got back, his room was a tip again. He asked his mum, "Did you mess my room?"
"No, what are you talking about?"

Rhys Lawson (9)
Langlands Primary School, Forfar

The Teddy Is Alive

One day, Dominic went to school and left his house dark and quiet. Suddenly, the teddy moved. It jumped down from the bed, then it walked downstairs. It had a tasty snack then used the iPhone 5 to take a selfie with the elf on the shelf. It then decided to do something naughty. It went into the bathroom and threw toilet paper all over the bathroom. It went with the elf upstairs. They played Crossy Roads on my phone and had another snack. They were happy with all the naughty things they had done and left it messy.

Dominic Pye (9)
Langlands Primary School, Forfar

The Dinosaur

Late at night, in Owen's kitchen, there was a battle between dinosaurs and soldiers. Some soldiers tried to kill a dinosaur, but the dinosaur killed them. It started with 50 versus 50, but five minutes later it became 20 versus 0. The dinosaurs won! Owen woke up and saw 100 pigs staring at him. They had fierce teeth. He shouted for his mum and dad but nobody came to help. He put his covers over his head. When he looked only some pigs were left. He fled his room and left the scary, terrifying house.

Owen Low (9)
Langlands Primary School, Forfar

The Escape

In the toy store there were millions of toys but there was one toy who wanted to escape. His name was Elephant. His friend was going to come with him, but just two days ago his friend disappeared. Elephant said, "I think he's gone to a new home. Has he gone?" Elephant decided to concentrate on his escape. He pounced off the shelf. He went in the vent and he didn't see the vent under him so he fell. Outside the shop a little girl saw him and picked him up. She thought he was cute and took him home.

Millie Stewart (9)
Langlands Primary School, Forfar

The Strange Glow

Once upon a time, there was a girl called Elly. She lived in a castle with her mum, dad, her big brother and sister. They went for a walk and Elly saw a strange glow. So she followed it and she saw it was a bottle of green stuff. Elly decided to drink it and fell into a deep, deep spell...

Someone walked past Princess Elly and kissed her on the cheek. She woke up and saw a handsome prince. They went to the castle and danced. After they danced, the prince asked the pretty princess to marry him.

Brooke Greig (9)
Langlands Primary School, Forfar

Wilomena's Dark Destruction

Once upon a time, there was a nasty, rich girl called Willow. One day she went to the toy shop, it was in the town. She saw a doll in the corner of the room, bought it and named it Wilomena. She got worn out with Wilomena after a while and put her in a toy castle. Wilomena was a haunted doll. She didn't like the castle at all. She planned to escape but first, she would do away with Willow! One night, Wilomena got a toy sword and climbed onto Willow's bed! Luckily Willow woke up and destroyed Wilomena.

Jessica Gibbs (9)
Langlands Primary School, Forfar

The Toys That Got Lost

One beautiful day, a girl was playing with her toys and then her mum shouted at her for tea. When she was gone her toys got up and played a game. A dog teddy called Star saw an elf called Snowflake sitting on the bed. Star asked her if she wanted to watch the fireworks outside. So Snowflake and Star watched from the window but then they fell into the garden. Snowflake said, "Since we are outside, let's go somewhere." They went on the roller coaster. It was amazing and they went on it again.

Hollie Stewart (9)
Langlands Primary School, Forfar

Under The Bed

Once there was a terrific, tremendous teddy bear who was scared of the dark, but it didn't help that he was stuck under the bed. He tried to get out from under the bed but there were too many boxes in the way. He waited until Boxing Day and eventually made it out. When Molly came back, she threw him back under the bed. He found a huge toy dinosaur, he tried to move it out but the box was too heavy. He found a huge drag back car and you will never guess what! He miraculously got through somehow.

Molly Brown (9)
Langlands Primary School, Forfar

Toys Go Crazy

When I was away my toys jumped out the toy box.
The chubby, soft, sparkly lion was the leader. All
the other toys were looking for a game to play.
They found a game but they didn't want to play it
so they ran. They ran all the way to my bed and
went under it. They found a notebook and a pen.
They drew a picture of themselves. Then when I
came back they were all scattered around. They all
froze. I knew they moved because the toy box was
open and there was a picture of them.

Charlie Davidson (9)
Langlands Primary School, Forfar

The Adventure Of A Lifetime!

On Saturday, I was playing in my room, but then I had to go for dinner. "Pintow, it's clear," whispered Ducky.

"Okay Ducky, but where is she?"

"I don't know."

"Thank you Mum!" I said.

"Oh no, she is coming, run!" shouted Ducky.

"I can't run remember, I have no legs!" Pintow screamed worried.

"Mmm, just... do something quick, hurry up Pintow!" yelled Ducky.

"I am trying, I am trying really hard!" But it was too late.

I walked into the room and saw him lying on the floor. "How did you get here?" I still don't know what happened.

Sheonagh Mitchell (10)
Milton Of Leys Primary School, Milton Of Leys

The Hungry Dog

Once upon a time, a little toy alien came to life!
The alien got eaten by a dog! "I have to save him,"
said Wonda the witch.
"Help!" came a voice from the belly of the dog.
"I know, I will do a magic spell," exclaimed Wonda.
"Well, hurry up," shouted Alfie the alien,
"Okay," yelled Wonda, "abracadabra."
"Did it work?" asked Alfie.
"No," said Wonda, "we can wait for him to poop or
make him sick."
"Wait for him to poop!" shouted Alfie.
"I will give him some food then," said Wonda...

Euan Douglas Learmonth (10)
Milton Of Leys Primary School, Milton Of Leys

Sad Santa Sighting

One snowy Christmas Eve, Poppy went on an adventure! She was decorating the house non-stop. The owners were totally confused! But as night fell she got mega tired. She went to sleep in the dog bed in the doll's house, even though she was a toy panda. But through the night she walked downstairs. She saw Santa. Her jaw dropped! She heard weeping, Santa was upset. She went to see him. "Are you okay?" she asked.

"No!" he snapped.

"What's up?"

"Nothing," he said sniffling. He dropped the presents under the tree. "Bye," he said. Poppy went to bed.

Katie Strachan (10)
Milton Of Leys Primary School, Milton Of Leys

Elfy The Elf

Elfy was a sad elf. But it was only recently that this happened because it was only just Christmas and everyone wanted the cool, new things, not a scabby baby's toy that had lost one arm. Elfy decided to run away. Out through the window, across the garden and she was free.
But little did she know that that night Tom cried, screaming, "Elfy!"
But Elfy did not hear because Elfy was already at the North Pole. Santa said, "Elfy, your owner is crying for you."
"Oh no, I better get back."
"He'll see you."
"Okay, I'll go back tomorrow."

Rhea Williams (10)
Milton Of Leys Primary School, Milton Of Leys

The Secret Unicorn!

"Bye Mum!"

"Okay, she's gone, let's have some fun." *Vroom! Vroom!* I love Molly's remote-control racing car. "Come with me, we're playing tig. You're it!" Oh, by the way, I'm Looloo, one of Molly's toys. I'm a unicorn. I think of Molly's dreams and then magically send them to her head so she has nice dreams. I just had a really good idea! Why don't we bounce on the beds, it will be really fun. Why don't we get my friend Toffee? "Yippee!" Uh-oh, Molly's back, got to go, bye.

Molly Fitzpatrick (10)
Milton Of Leys Primary School, Milton Of Leys

The Toy That Was Left Behind

Once upon a time, there was a teddy called Rufus and he was left behind by his owner Milo at his granny's house. One night Rufus was awoken by the terrifying sound of a creaking door. Jumping in fright, running into the darkness of the night, suddenly, something tapped him and yelled at the top of his voice, "Take me to the garden's spooky shed where all the others play at night."

"Where is that?" Rufus asked.

"I'll direct you," said the figure. Through the garden they heard some noise, the figure whispered, "Follow the noise..."

Lucy Mia McGibbon (10)
Milton Of Leys Primary School, Milton Of Leys

Present Opening

The magical time was here. Evie sprinted downstairs, then peeked at her majestic presents. The excitement was unbearable. A bright light shone on a red and green toy. An amazing elf was sat there. Evie tiptoed through her giant living room and ripped open her wonderful presents. Her loving family rushed down to feel joy flooding through their bodies. Evie grabbed her tiny elf and shrieked, "Merry Christmas!" The little elf smiled, then they both opened the presents rapidly. Evie's mum and dad got the old camera and watched closely. Evie hugged the tiny elf tightly.

Mia Croall (10)
Milton Of Leys Primary School, Milton Of Leys

The Crazy Fidget Spinner!

One night, the crazy fidget spinner started to destroy the house. It was Christmas Eve, the child was sleeping as the fidget spinner spun violently through the walls and ceilings...
The next morning, it was Christmas Day. The child woke up but he was so cold because the house was destroyed! Suddenly, the child ran to his mum and said, "The house is gone!" but Santa still came so he opened his presents. They went to their granny's house to stay. The fidget spinner was never found.
One month later, they got their house back and it was New Year.

Cara Cuthbert (10)
Milton Of Leys Primary School, Milton Of Leys

The Slime That Stole Christmas

One Christmas Eve, Slimey the toy was going to steal Christmas from everybody. Slimey's plan was to ruin Christmas and steal all the presents, but Slimey didn't have hands to pick presents up, so Slimey had to roll over presents so they stuck to him. "Finally... time to steal the presents." Off Slimey went to ruin Christmas. Slimey entered my room on Christmas morning and was upset, I wondered what was wrong. He was upset because he felt bad for what he had done, so he returned all the presents to everybody and they all had a holly jolly Christmas!

Kirstie Munro (10)

Milton Of Leys Primary School, Milton Of Leys

Mission Tucker

One dark, scary night I heard a creak in the ground. Carefully I looked under my bed. "Aah!" Phew! It was only Tucker the teddy. My dad had given me Tucker for my birthday. Suddenly, my elbow caught on my magic dust. I whispered to myself, "Oh no, this can't be good."
Then Tucker came alive and started talking to me. He screamed, "Wanna come out for a fly?"
"Of course!" I shouted. So that night we both went out on an extraordinary ride and since then we go out every night and we are now amazing friends forever.

Carla Quigley (10)
Milton Of Leys Primary School, Milton Of Leys

The Magical Book

Besides the book called 'Awful Auntie', my mum said it's time to go so I said, "Can I bring my book with me?"

She said, "Yes." So I went upstairs to get it.

Six hours later, we arrived at Blackpool and went to our hotel room, number 315, and brought our suitcases in and got set up. Mum said, "Time to read."

I said, "Okay." I read ten pages of my book called 'Awful Auntie'. I think about it in my head too much and I become the awful auntie! I don't know why it happened...

Chloe Ironside (10)
Milton Of Leys Primary School, Milton Of Leys

The WW2 Adventure

One day Aimee was playing with her favourite toy Holly, and then she had to go out! But while Aimee was away, her toys came to life! "We should have an adventure!" explained Molly.

"Okay," said Sparkles. Sparkles was Aimee's other toy. They time travelled back to WW2. They were amazed! Molly loved it but Sparkles didn't. They saw Winston Churchill. There was bombing going off from Germans as well. Molly said they should go home! When they got back to the bedroom, Aimee was just home. They were happy to be home.

Aimee Cameron (10)

Milton Of Leys Primary School, Milton Of Leys

The Dangerous Mission

It was Christmas morning and Timmy got a box of chocolates. He placed it on top of his cabinets. Timmy's toys became jealous. Three of his toy soldiers with green and black face paint had a plan to get the chocolate! Timmy fell asleep, then the soldiers acted out their plan. They slowly climbed up the cabinets but one of the soldiers fell down with a yelp. His body made a bang! Timmy rolled over with a yawn but he never awoke. The two soldiers felt relieved. They went up the handles, jumped into the chocolates and had a feast.

Ben Murdoch (10)
Milton Of Leys Primary School, Milton Of Leys

Mysterious Teddy Bear

One day, my mum told me we would go to the toy store next week if I was good. I was jumping with joy. "Yeah! I can't wait..."
The day finally came. I was up as fast as possible. "I am up! I am up!" My mum is still in her bed.
"Let's go to the toy store, come on!" I shouted in her ear and up she got.
"Let's go," groaned my mum. Off we went to the toy store.
I shouted, "I am getting a teddy bear." We got the teddy bear, suddenly the eyes turned red. "Aaah!"

Shaun Clare (10)
Milton Of Leys Primary School, Milton Of Leys

The Great Race

The race was on, I drove my speeding Nissan R34-GTR Skyline in front of the Corvette, into first I go! After I'm through the Barbie mansion, the finish line is in sight. I got through the mansion, however, the track changes, it's now a humongous loop-the-loop into a ramp. This is it... I hit the nitrous, shift up and speed! I keep thinking I need the prize of 1,000,000 gummy bears. Then suddenly, I see the Corvette on my tail. I try swerving around to lose his quick car, but then it's neck and neck... It ends.

Zach Evans (10)

Milton Of Leys Primary School, Milton Of Leys

Toy Goes Missing

One mysterious day, I had a funny feeling about my toys, they were shaking then I went to the loo. "Hey, I really want to go to the NBA so let's go," whispered Lebron James.
"I'm going to play with my toy, hey where is it?" shouted Ben.
So Lebron went to NBA. "I went on my bike."
"Hey, there he is!" shouted Ben, so he crept on the kerb, I grabbed Lebron James so we walked on the pavement to the bike and we came back home. Then I went to bed and slept.

Jamie Hamilton (10)
Milton Of Leys Primary School, Milton Of Leys

The Bobble Head

One magical day a toy bobble head came to life and was stuck in the car. Obviously, he wanted to get out. After jumping onto the car seat, the toy went to the back seat. The toy saw a back seat window open, he climbed up the car seat and jumped out the window and cracked his arm. It had fallen off, he took his arm with his other arm and threw it under the garage door and he got past. He met another toy. "Hi Bobble Head, do you have a name?"

"Yes, it is Bob."

"Mine is Toby."

Karlis Rozenbahs (10)
Milton Of Leys Primary School, Milton Of Leys

The Battle Of Five

One day five toy soldiers had to go on a mission. The mission was to capture an enemy tank. It was a daring mission so they set out looking in all directions in case of an ambush or booby traps. John the sniper heard some rustling in the bushes. It was an enemy platoon of ten. *Bang! Bang! Bang!* A battle broke out. But after hours of tense fighting, the conclusion came... "Let's be friends!" they all shout."Yeah!" they cried out in happiness. They did not get the tank but they did get friends.

Ethan Allan Rae (10)
Milton Of Leys Primary School, Milton Of Leys

Bunny And Her Rapunzel Adventure

One freezing night, a worn-out old bunny suddenly came to life. She jumped up ready to see her friends. Bunny was frightened to jump from the massive bunk bed so she found bits of old tissue and tied them together. Bunny pretended she was Rapunzel. She climbed down and suddenly a quick spark came and washed her away to a castle. She called for help but nobody came. She sighed and let her hair drop down, she saw the sun rising. She tried to get out. But then she saw a hole, climbed out and got to the bunk bed.

Rachel Sharp (9)
Milton Of Leys Primary School, Milton Of Leys

The Toy World!

"Girls come on, while Summer is at football we need to hide from crazy Lotty," said Anna.
"Hi, do you want to come and play with me?" Lotty said.
"No thanks Lotty, we have to go and get our nails done," muttered Kathleen. So everyone except Lotty went to get their nails done. They saw a shadow and it was Summer! The girls started to run and run, but they could not get anywhere. Summer caught up with them, picked them up and threw them into the box, but how could they get out...?

Neve Crawford (10)
Milton Of Leys Primary School, Milton Of Leys

Amazing Football!

The amazing football... all he wanted to do was be the football in the World Cup Final. That was his dream. He's now six and the World Cup is every four years. The World Cup starts in July and it's now June, he hopes it will be Portugal V Spain in the final because he really wants to meet Ronaldo and Matra. He lives in Manchester. The final is in London, he's never been to London.

The next day, the referee picked him and his dream came true but it was Portugal V Brazil but he got to see Ronaldo!

Cole Cameron (10)

Milton Of Leys Primary School, Milton Of Leys

Candy Queen Mistake

It all started when I was cleaning the loft. I found an old box of dolls, Among the other Barbies, one of them stood out against the rest. My old candy queen doll. I showed my mum the doll and went to put it where I found it.

The next morning I woke up to see gummy bears on the ceiling! For breakfast, Mum made me M&M's! I went through to the living room to find a girl I didn't recognise. I chased her around until she finally turned back into a doll. That's the story about the candy queen.

Emma Bowsher (10)
Milton Of Leys Primary School, Milton Of Leys

The Diabolical Slime Factory!

One blazing day, the toys on the shelf shifted onto the floor. "Okay, he's left, let's go!" explained a teddy. They were planning on making a slime factory. The toys began to collect materials for the diabolical slime factory.

"Go, go, make it snappy folks, we need wood, metal, wool, anything," yelled an army soldier. Now the structure was formed on the carpet. Fidget spinner began to spin the soon too slimy slime. But then Jeff came in and he was shocked to see a massive slime factory.

Sam Kinnear (10)
Milton Of Leys Primary School, Milton Of Leys

Toy Soldiers

Last night I was lying in my creaky bed when I heard something quiet. I didn't want to look... but I did.

A few minutes later, I cautiously looked under my bed, although I didn't want to look. But I did and saw green toy soldiers.

After I saw them I shot back up with shock. Not long after I leaned over my creaky bed to see. I started talking quietly in case I woke anyone up. They stopped being vicious and started being kind. I got tired and went to sleep but when I woke up, they were gone.

Theo Cartwright (10)
Milton Of Leys Primary School, Milton Of Leys

Fidget The Wind-Up Mouse

Once upon a time there was a wind-up mouse called Fidget who lived with his owner Eilidh. During the day Eilidh plays with her favourite toy, Fidget and after the very long day, when Eilidh goes to bed, Fidget comes alive and eats Eilidh's stinky socks. The stinky sock juice gives him so much energy! He can run around the world twice in just one night, making sure he gets back before Eilidh wakes up. When she plays with Fidget she does not know why he smells of stinky socks or why her socks keep disappearing too!

Sophia Loates (10)

Milton Of Leys Primary School, Milton Of Leys

The Toy Santa

One night on Christmas I said to Santa I would like a mini Santa. I got in bed and the next morning I quickly opened the present. "Oh, it's a mini Santa, but something is wrong, I think his arm just moved! and I saw it again and it's talking to me! This is the best present I ever got in my life!" My Santa was my best friend and we talk, play and watch movies, but when I got older, I did not play with Santa any more. I stopped believing in Santa and mini Santa disappeared.

Christopher Buchanan (10)

Milton Of Leys Primary School, Milton Of Leys

The Bad Football Player!

Last week, I was eating dinner but there was an odd sound like gas leaking but it was very continuous. I went upstairs but I couldn't see anything at all.

A few hours later, I heard another noise coming from upstairs so I went up to check and I couldn't believe what I saw... It was my whole room trashed, all I could see was ripped-up paper. The culprit was my right back player from my football game. I made him clean up all the mess. It took us three hours to clean up but we did it.

Caleb Dowling (10)

Milton Of Leys Primary School, Milton Of Leys

The Revenge Of Metal-Head

One day a young boy bought a toy robot. He played with it every day but a week later he got a new alien toy and didn't play with the robot anymore. Sneakily, one day, when the boy was outside playing with his other toys, the robot came to life and set a trip wire up on the door. Happily the boy came sprinting back inside, he fell and dropped his new toy alien and it smashed to pieces all over the white shining floor! The robot smiled when the boy finally played with him once again.

Joel Sleet (10)
Milton Of Leys Primary School, Milton Of Leys

The Annoying Furby!

One foggy, snowing night I was just about to brush my teeth, when suddenly I heard flapping. I turned around and saw two glowing eyes. It was my Furby. I was very scared, then it spoke to me and said, "Hi, Keryn, how are you?" I did not know what to say. I was speechless. I said hi but I was scared. I just went to bed. But in the middle of the night she just kept on waking me up, so I put her in a box.

The next few days she became less annoying. I love her now.

Keryn Maclean (10)
Milton Of Leys Primary School, Milton Of Leys

The Pig And The Dog.

One Sunday, the toys' owner went to town and that is where the magic begins. It was a normal day for the toys and a normal day for the owner too. But what the owner didn't know was that toys could move. The toy pig got up and realised the door was open! He saw a big dog staring at the pig and that wasn't good because it was the dog's toy. As the dog came at the pig, a big black shadow came with it. The light went on as the owner came in looking confused.

Calvin Barrie Cornthwaite (10)
Milton Of Leys Primary School, Milton Of Leys

Angry Bird

One day my owner left the house to go to the shop. But suddenly, I came alive. This was where the adventure began. I was in my old, rusty bed when suddenly I heard soldiers. I was worried but I made friends with the soldiers and we made a hotel but it exploded and I lost three of my soldiers. But that was okay, I also made a car so that I could get around the house more quickly. Suddenly, I heard a car outside and it was my owner's car, so I had to go to bed.

Owen Anderson (10)
Milton Of Leys Primary School, Milton Of Leys

Cupcake The Bear

One sunny day, me and my owner were at the beach, then her mean sister kicked me into the cold water! My arms were flapping like no tomorrow, then suddenly, a seagull grabbed me! He flew to a forest near my home. His yellow beak slipped and I fell into a toy fairy village where the fairy toys helped me by giving me a flight back home. I got in through the letterbox and ran up the stairs, walking into my owner's room and slept for the rest of the night.

Keira Broadfoot (10)
Milton Of Leys Primary School, Milton Of Leys

Party In Igloo

One night all of my toys came to life and they snuck downstairs and opened the back door. It creaked, then all the toys went into the snow and had a snowball fight. After the snowball fight, they went on the trampoline and in the morning I spotted them on the trampoline, then one of them spoke. I hurried downstairs to tell my mom and dad, they did not believe me. They told me to go back to sleep, but I did not listen to what they said. It was very fun.

Tristan Crook (10)
Milton Of Leys Primary School, Milton Of Leys

The Great Draw

This is Manchester City Vs Chelsea at the Etihad Stadium. What a goal," cried Jeff. Agüero makes it 1-0 Manchester City. "I am better than you," giggled gold unlimited addition Sergio Agüero. "No you're not!" said 100 club Eden Hazard! Half-time. "Right, let's do some training," said the manager.
Agüero passes to 100 club Debrune. "I'll kick off," said Jeff. "What a goal for Chelsea," said Jeff. Hazard makes it 1-1.
"Full time," said the ref.
"I'm sorry," said Hazard.
"I'm sorry too," said Agüero.
"So can we be friends?" asked Hazard.
"Yes," said Agüero, "let's play football."
"Okay."

Callum Mckay (9)
Our Lady's RC Primary School, Perth

Haunted Toys

One Halloween two girls went trick or treating. They went outside and got loads of sweets until they got to the most scariest house in the world. They crept past and knocked on the door. "Who's there?" whispered one of the girls.
"Do you think anyone is there?"
"No, do you?" and ran away and bumped into Abigail and ghosts! Abigail grabbed the two girls and locked them up, Abigail dropped the key.
"Look, the key!" said one of the girls, "Come on, let's go home." They ran as fast as they could. "I'm never celebrating Halloween again, bye-bye."

Sophie Rigby (8)
Our Lady's RC Primary School, Perth

The Brother Toy Soldiers

"Leo, Leo," shouted Bob.

"We can play all night long, Bob, watch out, a vortex," yelled scared and loudly Leo.

Bob and Leo tumbled through the vortex, landed with a thump on the Land of Soldiers. Leo panicked, Bob didn't panic.

"This is awesome!" shouted Bob.

"This is not awesome, we have to go back to the toy shop!" shouted Leo.

"Let's go to the pit," said Bob.

"No," replied Leo, "let's go, let's find the vortex cave, it's a month-long journey. Oh my gosh," said Leo.

"Finally, let's go home now."

Jan Jaromir Kruczynski (8)
Our Lady's RC Primary School, Perth

Lost Num Noms

Barbie and Fairy were in the forest. Barbie went, "Boo," to the fairy.

"Why did you do that?" said the fairy.

"Sorry, I was looking for my Num Noms," explained Barbie.

"Do you want help?" asked the fairy.

"Yes please," said Barbie. They went looking for the Num Noms, then they went into the plane to go look for them.

The fairy said, "They aren't there, let's go on the boat." They realised that the Num Noms were gone forever.

"I am so sad," said Barbie.

The fairy said, "Don't cry. Sorry, they are gone."

Shayla Mangan (9)
Our Lady's RC Primary School, Perth

Yasmin And Evil Yandere Chan

Melissa the cat, Yasmin the cat and Yandere Chan were all in the woods. "What a lovely day." "Hello there Yasmin," giggled Yandere Chan. "Why are you laughing? I don't like this, I don't feel comfortable," Yasmin cried. She ran off, then she got lost and she found a school. She went inside and she went in the bathroom and she locked herself in. *Smash! Smash! Boom! Bang!* "What is this?" yelled Yasmin. Yandere Chan smashed the bathroom door Yasmin was shocked when she saw her. She was twitching. What was wrong with her?

Karolina Maraszkiewicz (8)
Our Lady's RC Primary School, Perth

The Dead Doll

One day, Barbie and Ken went to the graveyard but when it got dark a scary dead doll came out of the ground. Barbie screamed. "It's okay," whispered the doll. "My name is Dotty."
"Oh hi," laughed Barbie.
"Please come with me," begged the doll as she explained about the evil god taking over her life. So off they went to the evil god.
At first the evil god was mad but then he felt bad for the doll and sighed, "You are now not under my spell."
Then the doll said, "Thank you for everything and bye-bye."

Laura-Marie Barzey (9)
Our Lady's RC Primary School, Perth

The Talking Football

It was a dark and cold night. Jimmy was a talking football, though he wished he had legs until one day, a boy came with his mum. "Mummy, Mummy, I found a football," cried the boy, and when he got there all he saw was friendly faces.

"Can you get me some legs?" asked Jimmy.

"No, sorry, we don't have any here," said a fat teddy.

"But we'll take you to the clinic," said a pig.

"Okay," said Jimmy.

When he came back from the clinic he was way more than happy. He had legs!

Chloe Geddes (9)
Our Lady's RC Primary School, Perth

Mario

"Mario, Mario," shouted Luigi.
"What is it?" mumbled Mario.
"There's a massive black hole," said Luigi."
"Oh no," said Mario. They fell in it. Luigi landed in Perth and Mario landed in China. Bowser followed Luigi, Luigi saw him and knew the only way was the crown jewels to get home. Bowser and Luigi knew it was a race to get the crown jewels. Back in China, Mario got an aeroplane. Bowser caused lots of trouble. Luigi got the crown jewels, they all teleported back.

Ben Brown (8)
Our Lady's RC Primary School, Perth

Once Upon A Toy

"Sophie, remember to tidy your room," shouted Mum. So Sophie started to tidy her room. Once she was finished, she found two very old dolls she had never seen before. When Sophie went to sleep her toys came alive. They went to go and play at the park but one of the dolls got lost.

The next day, the girl's room was extremely messy. But the doll was still lost. When she had finished tidying again, she found the missing doll. That night, the dolls did not come to life, they had just turned back into normal dolls.

Ciara Rowe (8)
Our Lady's RC Primary School, Perth

WWE Figures' Adventures

"Get me out of here!" shouted all the WWE figures. They all fell off the shelf into a vortex and shouted, "Aahhh," and landed. All of a sudden, they landed in a toy shop. They quietly crept up and down the aisle and looked for the vortex to take them home. Later that day it all happened again but they didn't want to go home because they had so much fun. They played with the toys and played lots of games such as tig and other games. The sun started to rise, they started to run to the vortex.

Maddy Taylor (8)
Our Lady's RC Primary School, Perth

Soldiers Ahoy

Once there was a soldier army in a toy shop. In the toy section there were lots of soldiers but then one of the soldiers fell out and then a kid stamped on the soldier. Then the soldier cried, "Ow." The army finally found the very broken soldier. The shop closed then suddenly, all the toys came alive. Then all the toys went crazy. However, the manager forgot his keys so he got a weird surprise. There were toys all over the place. There were soldiers in the football tub, also the computers.

Jack Anderson (8)
Our Lady's RC Primary School, Perth

The Living Soldiers

The boy was at school and the soldiers were training. After school, the boy ran upstairs and saw his toy moving. "Maybe I was just seeing things." Later that day, the boy went out to play but the cat got in and didn't like that so they had a war and no one won. But after an hour the boy came back and saw the cat and the soldiers fighting and he took the cat back out and put all his toys back and got ready for bed. It got dark and the birds sang all night.

Jayden Long (8)
Our Lady's RC Primary School, Perth

Jeffy The Lazy Toy

One day a toy called Jeffy was sitting on the shelf, then out of nowhere, a mysterious bright light shone. Jeffy got sucked into it, "Aah!" shouted Jeffy, he landed on a planet-looking object. Jeffy saw a man in white, he gave Jeffy a sword. A disgusting looking alien came up to Jeffy and the alien's head got cut off. Jeffy took a mysterious gun and fired a laser at an alien. Its head came off. After ten hours of work they won. They all went on the rocket back to Earth.

Ross Middleton (9)
Our Lady's RC Primary School, Perth

Magical Toy

Once there was a soldier, he was a toy. He didn't do much, but one day a magical fairy made him a real soldier but he had to get out of the house. He got out of the house, no problem. So now he was a real soldier, he could apply for a job. So he thought he could work for the army, but was not strong, so he went to the gym. Then he went back to the military base and he was the fittest in the whole army, but the alarm went off. There was a false alarm.

Kayden Netherington (8)
Our Lady's RC Primary School, Perth

The Evil Elf

There was a boy called Jaxon. He was at his house and all of a sudden, he saw his elf had turned evil. "Oh no," shouted Jaxon. The elf was chasing him up the stairs, but Jaxon hid under his bed. Jaxon stayed quietly under his bed for a while until Santa came down the chimney and helped Jaxon and found the elf. Santa took him to his workshop and changed him back to being a good elf again. They lived happily ever after.

Millie Roache (8)
Our Lady's RC Primary School, Perth

The House

As the tiny army men walked towards the cold house, Storm Magma thundered over them. Suddenly, a speedy lightning strike hit the house, then burst into flames. Then a scream came out of the house. "Soldier Three," shouted the general, "we have to get in there."

"We can't get through there," Soldier Two said, shivering.

"Come on Soldier Two, get a grip." As they were running to the voice of Soldier Three, two sizzling red eyes followed them. Then the general and Soldier Two reached Soldier Three. An enormous creature's shadow appeared and the creature ate them in one piece.

Eilah Sophie Win (9)
Portlethen Primary School, Portlethen

Attack!

"It's time to go," said Soldier 1, and they got the parachutes to dive down on the enemies. "3, 2, 1, dive." *Whoosh!* They fell and fell and landed on a wooden floor.
"Get the ropes out," said Soldier 2. They hooked the ropes into the bed and hauled them all up. "Attack!" *Bang! Crack! Boom!*
"Help," said Soldier 5 who was being lifted to get thrown to the floor. "Ouch!" He had been broken.
"Oh no, we need the cannon." So five soldiers wheeled the cannon, but too late, the gigantic hand had swept them to the floor. "Ouch!"

Jacob Arthur Saum (9)
Portlethen Primary School, Portlethen

The Elf On The Shelf

"Time to go Christmas shopping," said Tom's mum. "Why don't you get that elf?"
"Okay, let's get it."
"Time to go home. "Time for bed," said Tom's mum.
"Okay, it's clear," said the elf. "I better go hide on the Christmas tree."
"Time to wake up Tom, where's the elf?"
"He was on my shelf, let's go find him Mum! It's going on top of the Christmas tree."
"Tom, it's Christmas Eve tomorrow. Wake up Tom, there's a note from the elf and it says 'Merry Christmas'."

Lewis Scotson (10)
Portlethen Primary School, Portlethen

Operation Sloth

"There was our last call for our flight," shouted Sam's mum. Sam had a toy sloth called Neil, Neil was so precious to Sam and he was so cuddly and fluffy. When Sam was running to his gate Neil fell off the suitcase. Sam didn't realise and went to the gate. Neil then magically came to life and went to the wrong gate and the cabin crew didn't notice Neil. He was then transported to first class and then a lady came over. It was Sam's mum and she said, "They were on the wrong flight, not Neil."

Lola Phillips-Johns (10)
Portlethen Primary School, Portlethen

The Lego Chaikters

One day, there was Lego Batman, Santa, Spider-Man, the Hulk and Superman, they were fighting together. All of them were strong. Hulk punched Batman's face and sometimes they steal snacks like biscuits, sweets and chocolate. Santa sends presents to everyone. Most of the time they come down the stairs and fight. The Hulk wins most of the time and then they watch TV, but most of the time they do not know how the TV works. Spider-Man uses webs more than Superman flies. Everyone finished eating snacks, then it was bedtime.

Andrew Liam Brown (9)
Portlethen Primary School, Portlethen

The Great Escape

The lonely teddy bear had a plan, a very mischievous one indeed. He was always bored sitting on the bed all the time, so his plan was adventure! His great escape! First he would journey down the gigantic wooden ladder. He started his journey at the top of the ladder where there was a long drop down. He thought about it for a moment, then took one great leap on to the first step, then the second but before he got to the third step, his owner walked in and the next thing he knew, he was back in bed.

Lacey May Murray (11)
Portlethen Primary School, Portlethen

The Car And Motorbike

The black car wanted to race the motorbike in the kitchen. When they were ready they started like lightning and the car tried to push the motorbike into the sink but they both weren't looking where they were driving. They jumped off a counter and landed in an oven with a turkey and stayed there for one hour until it was time for dinner. Someone said, "Ouch! What's this?" looking at the car and motorbike, holding his broken, chalky tooth after he bit on the black car in his yucky food.

Alex Proszynski (9)
Portlethen Primary School, Portlethen

Fluffy The Unicorn

Fluffy had one dream, to be a real unicorn. Then one day a miracle happened. She was a real unicorn. She went into the forest but there was one problem, she kept tripping over. She sat on a tree stump crying. "I wish I was a toy again," said Fluffy.

The next morning, she realised she was not in the forest, but her next-door neighbour's back garden. Now she had to get back to her house. But another problem, there was a dog. This was an evil dog. It got Fluffy's head off!

Eva Brownie (10)
Portlethen Primary School, Portlethen

The Disco Monkey

At Toy Land there was a disco going on. There was a monkey running the disco and all toys were invited. It was awesome until a party pooper came in, Miss Sassy Unicorn. As soon as she walked in all Mr Monkey saw were soldiers guarding her and everyone was frozen. She even had a fluffy Chihuahua. It was so cute. Then everyone unfroze and Mr Monkey and everyone carried on with the disco. It was cool once again in the disco until the light turned on and everyone went back to the toy box.

Ellis J Harrison (9)
Portlethen Primary School, Portlethen

The Werewolf

In the forest there was a tiny house. A toy wolf crept into the house and he was so tired he went to his bed. In his dream he was speaking French and he was a pig. In his back garden he had toy chickens and he ate all of them. Then he turned into a toy chicken and went to the forest. It went to his tree house and saw his dog. His dog got a fright and then he died because he got such a fright. The wolf-chicken was so sad and he woke up from his dream.

Sophia Le Tissier (9)
Portlethen Primary School, Portlethen

The Escape From War

The sergeant looked around the corner and said, "Duck!" and everyone ducked.

Some soldiers were in a helicopter and they shouted, "Fire!" A few soldiers got shot and died and some families needed to go to funerals and were extremely upset. While they were at the funeral, Thomas stepped on all the soldiers and families that were there. He lifted his foot and saw all of them on the floor. They were crushed!

Miya Skea Bowes (9)
Portlethen Primary School, Portlethen

The Kong Terror!

C'mon, build me something so I can destroy it when you go away! thought Kong the toy gorilla. Owen built a Lego house and left for school. Kong woke up and he stomped towards the Lego house. He clenched his fists and he smashed the house. It was in pieces! Owen came home and he looked at his Lego house. He was upset for ages and it took Owen months to rebuild it.

Owen Smith (10)
Portlethen Primary School, Portlethen

Link's Mario Plush

Link's Mario plush comes to life in the morning or when he doesn't see him. He likes going on an adventure and playing video games. But one day, his owner Link came back and seeing his TV in his bedroom on he said, "How did my TV come on?" But then he turned it off and went for dinner. Link's Mario plush played video games while Link had his dinner.

Lewis Benjamin Archibald (9)
Portlethen Primary School, Portlethen

Pikachu

When I go to school my Pikachu comes to life. He goes downstairs and he can't figure out how to put on the TV, so he just watches the black screen. When he gets bored he climbs up my counter and eats snacks. When I'm at the doorstep he runs upstairs, he jumps on my shelf and stays like a statue...

Lewis Riddoch (9)
Portlethen Primary School, Portlethen

Clumsy And The 100 Soldiers

I'm Bo the narrator and this is the story of Clumsy Bear!

"Sergeant, all clear!" shouted Soldier One.

"Okay lads, tonight we must infiltrate the enemy!" roared Sergeant Ross. "Move out!"

"I got a new toy!"

"That's Andy," whispered Soldier 22. "Freeze!" he added. Andy came bursting through the door.

"Huh!" moaned Andy, "Sophia!" Andy sat his drone down and sped upstairs to get his sister.

"Can I play now?" said a booming voice.

"Clumsy not now!"

"But I'm a great soldier."

"Fine!" said Sergeant Ross.

"Yay!" he exclaimed. Clumsy went on to mess up everything the toy army did.

Rhys Deighan (11)
St Dominic's Primary School, Airdrie

Airobob's Adventure

It all began on a cold winter's day when Airobob flew for the first time. Suddenly, a Barbie attacked. "Aah!" screamed Airobob, "I'm under attack, help me. Barbie is awful! She nearly killed me and I can't fly ever again."
"Ha, ha, ha, you'll never fly again," laughed Barbie. Suddenly, he heard an engine, he was chuffed because he could fly. "Yippee!" shouted Airobob, "let's go for a journey to London!" However, the Barbie struck again. This time he never broke a wing - he landed in a house.
"What is that plane doing in my house?" shouted the lady...

Aiden Heafey (11)
St Dominic's Primary School, Airdrie

The Legend Of Pengie

One day, Christmas came and at Christmas all toys come alive and this is the story of Pengie. One day, Pengie said, "What? Where am I?" He looked right, he saw a star. He looked down, jumped and went downstairs, then he looked up and saw a reindeer and a sleigh outside the window. He saw an elf and Santa. "Santa," said Pengie quietly, "why are you here?"

Santa appeared in the house, "Have a merry Christmas," said Santa quietly. Suddenly, Pengie woke up, he checked downstairs for Santa. There were presents and a note saying, 'Merry Christmas Pengie'.

Szymon Kisiel (11)
St Dominic's Primary School, Airdrie

The Race-Off

"This is the greatest day of my life, I am racing every track I could possibly find and having fun with all my friends!" exclaimed Fury excitedly. Then suddenly Fury's owner burst through the door, holding a car.

"Zoom, zoom, this is my new favourite car!" said George. Fury was furious that he had been replaced by another car, so he decided to take revenge.

At midnight, Fury sneaked up to the car and whispered sharply, "This is my house, so we are going to race and whoever loses, leaves!" They pulled up to the starting line. 3, 2, 1...

Dawid Tomalka (11)
St Dominic's Primary School, Airdrie

A Barbie In Las Vegas

"This time again," bellowed Barbie, "I hate dark nights. I have to do something. I know what I'll do! I'll get my jet and move to Las Vegas, then go to the casino for Barbies and win some money, then I can buy my dream house in LA. I must go get my jet and take off for Las Vegas."

Finally! She was at the casino. "Let's win some money!" She stayed there for hours upon hours until she finally won the jackpot: $10,000,000. Then she threw her high heel at the person stealing her money and flew to LA.

John Michael Sweeney (11)
St Dominic's Primary School, Airdrie

Toy Military Mayhem

Tuesday the 31st of October. Ben the owner left the house.

Two hours later the toy men sent a threat claiming they were going to raid the military mayhem master's base. They explained that they will attack at 1300 hours. When Sergeant Bobert received the letter he had all of the Military Mayhem Masters lined up in rows of twenty, prepared for attack. At 1200 hours the toy men arrived. The toy men's Sergeant Doofinschmit was talking to Sergeant Bobert.

An hour later, the armies started fighting. There were a lot of men down. Then everyone dropped. Ben was home.

Rhys Brannan (11)

St Dominic's Primary School, Airdrie

The Journey Of The Forgotten

Beep, the robot, woke up to towers of rubble looming over him, his metallic red paint scratched and his buttons bashed. He examined the perimeter and saw toys and sweet wrappers. Beep moved his rusty gears, his old batteries chugging him on. It got denser and denser but he found his way out. He scanned the terrain... It was his owner's bedroom and he was under the bed. Once a loved toy, now forgotten. He felt weaker by the second, his batteries were failing. With one last breath, he saw a human shadow looming over him. It was his owner...

Michael Hunt (11)
St Dominic's Primary School, Airdrie

The Angel From Up Above

It was like any other day with snow, but little did Marco and Neve know that it wasn't a normal day. Suddenly, a roar came from upstairs. Marco and Neve spotted an angel and beside her a leopard. The angel took Marco and Neve to Heaven. They saw their gran and they gave her a hug and then they went back to the house, drank hot chocolate, made snowmen and snow angels. They went to bed and said goodbye.

Then in the morning, they opened presents and Angel and Coco were toys once more, then they vanished, or did they...?

Marco Russo (10)

St Dominic's Primary School, Airdrie

Barbie's Adventure

Barbie was in the doll's house and she was thinking. She had never been anywhere in the house except the bedroom! So while everyone was sleeping, she snuck downstairs. She saw the Christmas tree and she wanted to redecorate it so she took everything off - first, the baubles. She finished then went into the kitchen and saw all the food. She went into the fridge and got a chocolate bar. Then Barbie went upstairs and the owner of the house came in and saw the mess, then the toys heard a loud scream...

Leah Hamilton (11)
St Dominic's Primary School, Airdrie

Rocket's Great Escape

Once upon a time, there was a large toy called Olly. He had lots of different toys like pigs and cows, but he had a favourite. It was a raccoon called Rocket. Rocket didn't like Olly though, because he always bit him and threw him about. So one day Rocket decided to make a great escape. He waited until Olly started to eat his dinner, then Rocket made a mad dash. He ran for the windows because he knew he would fit through the window. He squeezed through one and he hit the cold air. He just kept running...

Ethan McGee (11)
St Dominic's Primary School, Airdrie

Buff Fred The Action Man

Once there was a boy called Steve. One day his mum shouted, "Dinner time and your room better be clean!" So he cleaned his room but forgot one toy - Buff Fred. So Buff Fred had to use his parachute to get to the other side of the room, but that got caught on the lamp, so he fell onto the bed. Soon after that, Steve came back upstairs, so Buff Fred ran to the cupboard and successfully made it! When Steve finally got up the stairs he said, "Why is Buff Fred's parachute on the ceiling lamp?"

Rhys McCarthy Railley (11)
St Dominic's Primary School, Airdrie

The Soggy Robot

Once there was a robot and every time the owner fell asleep, he came alive. However, any time he came alive he had nothing to do. Then one day he got so bored he went on an adventure! It was really hard - he had to jump shelves, drawers, toys and handles but he eventually got to the legendary hall. It was huge but the robot didn't fear, he looked around a little bit but then he slipped and fell down the stairs. He landed in the dog's water bowl. He fizzed, popped and blew up in a big bang...

Kai Stewart (11)
St Dominic's Primary School, Airdrie

Mischievous Teddy Bear

One day my mum told me to clean my room. I did and my mum came up. It was still a mess! Anxious, my teddy bear, had moved so I re-did it. I went into the hall to shout my mum and we both went back into my room. It was a mess again! "Leah, you're grounded!" said Mum and strangely, Anxious had moved again. *This is suspicious,* I thought. So I cleaned my room, hid my camera and got my mum. She went into my room, it was a mess. I got my camera. I couldn't believe my eyes...

Leah McCabe (11)
St Dominic's Primary School, Airdrie

Bank Mission

Far, far away, a brave little toy had a thirst for mischief, so went on a dangerous trip. That toy was Robbery Bob. So he got in his sparkly blue Mini and burst out the toy shop door. He had to hurry because it was midnight and people came to start up the tills at 5am. He drove to the bank, which was only ten metres away, so it didn't take long. He went in the bank, dodged lasers, jumped walls and got out with his money. While driving back, his roof caved in because he stole so much money...

Kerry McGill (11)
St Dominic's Primary School, Airdrie

A Day In The Life Of A Teddy

A day in the life of a teddy is much different to yours. They do all kinds of things... they like to have tea parties and dance sometimes. Here's a story of a teddy adventure.

One night, a teddy fell out of bed. He had to get back up but how? He went past the sweetie wrappers and through the spilt cola lake. He was sticky from walking through the cola but he was almost there. He started to climb the steps and was tired but soon he was back in bed and settled down to go back to sleep.

Jamie Shaw (11)
St Dominic's Primary School, Airdrie

Tommy Transformer

One morning when I woke up, I saw my toys and swords, Tom and Nikko lying all about the place, so I thought they were fighting. When I left the room my Transformers came to life. I didn't know but it's true, my toys came to life! Tommy was lonely. He needed a new friend. Happily, his dream came true. He made a friend called Jeff the minion. "Who are you?" asked Tommy.

"Jeff," shouted Jeff.

One day I even caught them playing at FIFA on my Xbox. They were best friends forever.

Liam Dunnery (8)
St Patrick's Primary School, New Stevenston

Hot Wheels

On a warm, sunny day, my Hot Wheels cars were racing on the track and there was a little crash. Other cars came in and they kept crashing and my Lego castle scattered everywhere. My mum came and said, "What a mess!" I went upstairs to my room and saw there was a big mess. I said, "It wasn't me."

But she said, "Who did it? The ghost car?"

I don't think she did believe me, that night when I went to bed I set a camera trap and saw it, then I showed my mum.

Josh Hutchison (8)

St Patrick's Primary School, New Stevenston

Henry The Football Player

When I returned from a big day at school, I went to my bedroom and it was a mess. I wondered who could have done it, then I checked all the rooms and they were not messed up. I went downstairs and I saw my football player on the shelf in my kitchen. I went up to my bedroom and it was messier than before Laughing with shock, I went downstairs to tell my mum. She said, "You are a silly Billy." I watched the TV until dinner and my bedtime, but then I saw my footballers outside...

Aiden Clarke (7)

St Patrick's Primary School, New Stevenston

Tom Cat

Tom the toy cat likes chocolate chip cookies and likes to be lazy all day, and he is very big and fat and he is green. One day he flew on holiday to Spain but then a crashed rocket fell on top of the plane and then the plane fell down to the North Pole. Tom then saw Santa and all the elves wrapping up the presents and then Santa came to Tom and gave him a present. Santa helped Tom Cat to fix his plane. Then he flew to Spain and when his holiday finished, Tom went back home.

Maksymilian Jablonski (8)
St Patrick's Primary School, New Stevenston

The Day Husk Was Naughty

One night during the summer, Husk sneaked out the room. He got ice cream from the kitchen and ate it. I found ice cream all near my bed and I wasn't eating it. So Husk must be magic and naughty. I took him out for a walk to give him fresh air because he had eaten too much ice cream. He was sick because of that ice cream. He felt so much better but he was all dirty. I went home and gave him a wash. He looked much better and he didn't eat any more ice cream.

Nikkita McAviney (8)

St Patrick's Primary School, New Stevenston

The Greedy Toy Rabbit

Last year I went to a park in Glasgow. Richard Rabbit jumped out of my bag! He loves to jump. Firstly he was eating all of my chocolate. Then he jumped all over the park and left a trail of glitter poo because of all the chocolate. Then we had to go to the vet because he was so full up of chocolate. The vet said he had to get an operation to get his belly cut open. The vet said he was a very greedy rabbit! For his punishment, he went to the gym with me and my brother.

Lisa McMonagle (8)
St Patrick's Primary School, New Stevenston

The Cat Who Loves Milk

One hot Friday when I woke up, I was going to eat my breakfast and I opened the fridge and my milk wasn't there. So I bought new milk. When I was going to eat my breakfast, I heard a noise from outside. My toy cat was snoring then I went inside and my milk wasn't there again. I heard a noise from upstairs so I ran up and there were cat footprints and the TV was on. Then I had a plan, I was going to set a milk trap the next morning to catch my cheeky toy cat.

Emmanuel Mathew (7)

St Patrick's Primary School, New Stevenston

Milly My Toy Pup

One night Milly my toy puppy went to the kitchen and got cookies. I heard a noise in the kitchen so I went downstairs to see. I saw my puppy eating cookies so I took her to my room until morning, but when I woke up she was not in bed. She was gone. So I looked in the kitchen but she was nowhere to be found, so I looked in the living room and eventually I found her in my mum's room and she had a spoon in her paw. What a very naughty pup she is!

Allanah Hall (8)
St Patrick's Primary School, New Stevenston

The Robot Slayers

On a dark night in November, Optimus Prime was guarding London Tower. Then Megatron appeared and started a fight with him. Optimus Prime's crew came along and jumped on Megatron. Optimus Prime said, "Take this Megatron." He fired lasers and rockets and then Megatron's crew came along and killed Bumblebee. Then Optimus Primes was so close to getting killed and Megatron was very angry.

Blair Carlyle (8)
St Patrick's Primary School, New Stevenston

The Magic Elf

In the middle of the night my toy elf, Buddy, came to life. He went to the kitchen, ate all the chocolate and threw a party. When I went downstairs, everything went quiet. I was scared, but then I saw Santa. He took Buddy to the North Pole to be taught some manners, and from that day on, I never saw the naughty elf, Buddy, again.

Hannah Margaret Doyle (7)
St Patrick's Primary School, New Stevenston

Est.1991

YOUNG WRITERS INFORMATION

We hope you have enjoyed reading this book – and that you will continue to in the coming years.

If you're a young writer who enjoys reading and creative writing, or the parent of an enthusiastic poet or story writer, do visit our website **www.youngwriters.co.uk**. Here you will find free competitions, workshops and games, as well as recommended reads, a poetry glossary and our blog.

If you would like to order further copies of this book, or any of our other titles, then please give us a call or visit **www.youngwriters.co.uk**.

Young Writers
Remus House
Coltsfoot Drive
Peterborough
PE2 9BF
(01733) 890066 / 898110
info@youngwriters.co.uk

 @YoungWritersUK    @YoungWritersCW